Mr. Bowltre's Madness

The Wand Chasers Book One

James Maxstadt

Mr. Bowltre's Madness

The Wand Chasers Book One

Printed in the United States of America

First Printing, 2022

ISBN: 9798835890125

James Maxstadt

Visit at jamesmaxstadt.com

Cover art and interior illustrations by Joe Covas

To Clara, who asked me to write a book for kids. And for Lou, who helped me come up with Mr. Bowltre and his crazy hair.

To Reeses Logan,

Magic is real!

Keep your eyes open...

Prologue

Danger walked the night. Strange, scary, crazy danger.

The creatures in the woods felt it and scurried away to hide until it had passed.

The trees seemed to feel it. The rustling of their leaves in the wind stopped.

Even the air seemed to sense it and fell still, without even the hint of a breeze.

Other things, too, stayed hidden as best they could. But, then again, they were designed— long ago— to eventually be found.

A strange shuffling made the only noise in the humid, summer night. It sounded as if one foot came down hard and then the other was pulled along behind. Slowly, the mismatched steps made their way into the woods and then continued along, seemingly aimless.

Moonlight brightened up the small section of forest enough that a shadow could be seen— if there had been anyone there to observe it.

Hunched shoulders, wild hair, and a lurching gait.

Whoever he was stopped and inhaled deeply through his nose, then growled low in his throat, making a harsh, wet sound.

"Here," he muttered. "It's here. Maybe more than one. I can smell it…"

He lifted his head and sniffed rapidly, as if trying to identify an elusive scent.

"Different," the man mumbled. "Something is different."

As if his words had energized him, the man became agitated. He suddenly took huge strides, pulling one leg behind the other, his head thrown back and sniffing, sniffing, always sniffing.

His foot stomped down into a low bush and a rabbit that had been hiding there, paralyzed by fear, suddenly broke cover and ran. The man's hand dipped inside his coat, and he jabbed something long and thin at the fleeing bunny.

A loud crack split the night and a bolt of lightning flashed from the object the man held. It hit the rabbit, leaving behind only bits of blackened fur.

The man snarled in disgust and put whatever he held back inside his coat.

"Ruined," he growled. He tilted his head back once more. "It's here. Somewhere. Something different. I'll find it, yet."

He continued on his way, stomping his left foot and dragging his right, until he was gone from the area.

Slowly, the air began to move again, the leaves rustled, and small animals stirred. None came near where the rabbit had met its end, though. And none crossed the path of the man who had stomped through their world.

Those other things stayed as they had been. Waiting for someone else.

Chapter 1

He was so bored that not even the sight of a baseball diamond could cheer Grayson up. A new town, no kids around that he could find, and now this. An overgrown, dusty, abandoned field, with scraggly weeds growing where there should have been mowed grass.

He kicked at the dirt near home plate. From there, he could see that the outfield just kind of ended up against the woods. Just right to have a ball get lost in if someone hit a homer.

Strangely, that thought lifted his spirits a little. Maybe there were a few balls in there, or even more than that. He might be able to find ten, or a hundred. Maybe a thousand! Hold on a minute. A thousand baseballs? From this sad excuse for a field? He didn't think so.

Still, he really might find a couple, so he set off toward the trees. His steps were much quicker than they'd been since coming to this town, where Dad had a new job and Mom was still unpacking. For the first time, he felt like *he* actually had something to do!

His enthusiasm didn't go away when he reached the edge of the woods. The trees were tall and cast long shadows everywhere, which was a welcome break from the hot sun. Beneath them, a whole bunch of scrubby bushes grew, thick with dark leaves, red berries that were no good to eat, and a whole bunch of thorns. It was going to be dangerous work to search for any lost baseballs.

"That's why they might still be there, I guess," he said aloud. But after a half-hour of searching, Grayson was just scratched, dirty, and tired.

Shade or not, it was a hot day. He hadn't found a single ball, which fit with everything else about this stupid new town they'd moved to.

He didn't know why they couldn't have just stayed where they were. He got it. Dad had a new job and Mom was looking for one here as well but was taking her time. She told Grayson that it was a great "opportunity" for them, whatever that was supposed to mean.

"You're eleven now," she'd told him. "You're old enough to understand that sometimes we have to do things that make sense, even if we don't like them at first."

He guessed he did understand that, but what was wrong with Dad's old—

"Ouch!"

He yelled, but he wasn't actually hurt. He'd just tripped over some stupid root or something and went down hard on his face. Luckily, he thought, he had cat-like reflexes and caught himself before he busted his nose. Although he hadn't been quick enough to stop himself entirely and was now sprawled on the ground.

He looked down to scowl at whatever had tripped him.

It *was* a root. . . sticking straight up about six to eight inches out of the ground and pointing at the tree branches like an accusing finger.

"You can't keep me here in the dirt!" Grayson imagined it saying.

But as he looked at it, he saw that it was less like a root than he'd first thought. For one, don't most roots just sort of come up to the surface and then right back into the ground, like a worm's back or something?

And didn't most roots have little hair-like things on them, where they were growing and pushing through the soil? And weren't they usually dirty and covered with bark that was ripping in places, maybe?

This thing was smooth and unblemished. It was dark wood, but without any bark, hairs, or dirt on it.

Grayson started to suspect that it wasn't a root at all.

He scrambled around so that his face was near it. He looked it up and down, but it didn't change.

"Not a root," he said. He wondered what it could be, then. "Only one way to find out," he muttered.

He wrapped his hand around it and pulled hard, expecting it to be stuck in the ground.

It slid free like the ground was giving it to him, making Grayson stumble backwards with a grunt.

Normally, that would have been annoying, but right then, he was more curious about what he now held.

Whatever it was, it was long and slender, with a carved handle that fit easily in his hand. Above that, the shaft was smooth and tapered to a dull point. Even after being in the ground, the whole thing was clean and shiny.

"A wand?" That's what it looked like anyway. "How did some kid's stupid toy wand end up stuck in the dirt in the woods?"

He guessed someone must have been playing a game... or maybe some bully had taken it from a smaller kid and buried it.

Grayson examined it more closely. Maybe it wasn't a toy, he thought. It was awfully nice. Maybe it belonged to some adult, and was like, a collectible thing. Like his Dad with his signed baseballs. Maybe, if he found the person it belonged to, he'd get a reward.

Maybe this day wasn't turning out so bad, after all.

He rose completely, still holding the wand, and looked around to make sure he was heading in the right direction.

Which was exactly when he realized that someone else was now standing on the baseball field.

Chapter 2

Whoever the person was, they were an adult.

Nothing unusual about that, Grayson told himself. It could be someone out walking their dog, although Grayson didn't see any pets.

It didn't really matter. He'd get out of the woods and go home, walking right past the person. If they said hello to him, he'd answer politely, but wouldn't stop. Grayson knew better than that. You didn't stop and have a conversation with a strange adult, not when you were totally alone, for sure.

Yep. Head home. Right now.

Only, Grayson found that his legs didn't want to move. He *could* move them, though. He figured that out when he looked down as he shuffled forward.

His movement, even though slight, was enough to rustle the bushes he was in.

The figure— a man from the looks of him— spun toward the sound, and Grayson noticed that he was slightly hunch-backed. The man's shoulders, covered by a long, dirty, black coat, were raised up near his ears. His back was curved so that his head jutted forward.

While that looked weird enough, it was the man's hair that surprised Grayson the most. It stood up in great spikes, all of which were colored either a bright green or bright yellow.

Grayson had never seen such hair on anyone, especially not on an adult.

The man seemed to be scanning the woods, looking for whatever had made the sound. He was far enough away that Grayson couldn't really see his face, but something told him that he didn't want the man to see him.

No, something didn't *tell* him; something *screamed* at him.

He stayed frozen, unsure of what to do.

He was being ridiculous. All he needed to do was take his new wand, walk out of the woods, and go home. Easy-peasy.

Except it wasn't. His feet still wouldn't move.

The man walked closer to the forest. He moved with a strange limp, taking a step and dragging the other leg forward. All the time, he kept his head moving back and forth, searching for something.

He *was* searching for Grayson.

Grayson knew that as sure as he'd ever known anything in his life.

And he knew again that he didn't want that man to find him.

Closer now, and Grayson could see that the man had eyes that bulged so far out that Grayson didn't know how they could ever close. Maybe they didn't. Maybe they stayed open all the time, staring and searching. Maybe that's all this guy did.

He stared and he searched and when he found a kid he grabbed them and pulled them to him where he opened his mouth filled with sharp teeth and—

Something hit Grayson hard. He went down with a crash in the bushes and a hand pressed over his mouth, stifling his yell of surprise.

"Stay down!" A voice whispered in his ear. "What are you? Stupid?"

Chapter 3

Grayson struggled in the grip of whoever had a hold of him, but he wasn't able to get away. Whoever it was, they were stronger than he was.

"I said to be quiet!" The voice hissed in his ear again. This time, Grayson noticed that it was a girl's voice.

He stopped struggling. It was bad enough being held down like a helpless baby, but to have a *girl* do it? It was better to look like he was cooperating.

"Are you done?" she whispered.

Grayson nodded, and, after another couple of seconds had passed, the girl moved her hand away and let go of him.

He was about to spring to his feet when he heard the snapping of twigs nearby and that same sense that had told him it would be bad— really bad— to have that strange man see him, told him to stay perfectly still now.

Grayson froze. Behind him, the girl did the same.

The man with the crazy hair and googly eyes was coming right toward them. Grayson could hear him moving through the bushes. Stomp, drag, stomp, drag.

Crazy-hair stopped a few feet away. Grayson shifted the tiniest bit so that he could look up, so that he could see the man's face.

He was looking right at him!

Those weird eyes, sticking too far out of the man's head, were focused directly on Grayson's own eyes!

He drew in a breath, but the girl behind him touched him gently on the shoulder. Grayson held in the scream he'd been about to let loose.

The man stared at him for a moment more, then his eyes began to rove around again. He was still searching for him. Somehow he hadn't seen Grayson after all.

But then, the man stopped moving entirely, except to tilt his head back. His lips curled and his nose twitched. Grayson realized that the man was now sniffing the air, trying to find him by smell.

Suddenly, the man's head snapped back down, his yellow and green hair shaking like trees in the wind and spun back toward where Grayson was hiding. His lips parted again, this time in a wicked smile that showed brown teeth.

"I know you're here, boy," he snarled.

His voice sounded like dogs fighting. He growled and it was harsh and wet, like the man was about to slobber all over his own chin.

"You might as well come out and give it to me. It's mine anyway. You're stealing. And you know what happens to stealers, don't you? They're wicked. They must be punished."

The girl's hand tightened on Grayson's shoulder at the same time his own hand tightened around the wand, which he'd almost forgotten he was still holding.

This? This is what the man wanted? Why hadn't he just said so? He could have just called out and told Grayson that he'd lost something and Grayson would have gladly given it to him.

But to stand up now? To be close to that evil face and those eyes…

Grayson couldn't do it.

The man shuffled a step closer. Stomp, drag.

"I can smell it, boy. Because it's mine. They're all mine. Now—"

There was a sudden loud crack, deeper into the woods. The man spun around with surprising quickness, and his hand darted inside his filthy, black coat. When it came out, he held a wand much like the one Grayson still clutched, except that his was made out of some black wood, with a bright golden line running along it.

The man jabbed it forward, like he was pointing it at something Grayson couldn't see and shouted a word.

"Lectrician!"

Or something like that. With the man's harsh, wet voice, Grayson couldn't really tell what the word was.

What he did know, though, was that lightning suddenly shot from the end of the wand. Grayson heard the sharp frizz of it and the splintering of something off in the woods.

The loud cracking sound came again. The man growled and started to move away, still staring into the woods at something far off. He let loose with another lightning bolt.

It wasn't until it had happened a third time, sounding much farther away now, that the girl finally stood up.

"Come on," she said, without even looking at him. "We have to go."

Chapter 4

Grayson jumped up but didn't immediately follow the girl.

When she noticed that he hadn't, she turned back to face him. She was about his own age, he guessed, with freckles across her pale nose. She was dressed in jeans and a t-shirt which were now dirty, with dead leaves stuck to them. More leaves were matted in her blond hair, which was tied back in a ponytail.

"What are you waiting for?" she asked.

"I'm not following you!" Now that the immediate danger of the strange man had passed, Grayson's calm was beginning to crumble. His legs felt shaky, his stomach hurt, and he felt his lower lip start to tremble.

He wasn't going to cry! Not with anyone— especially a girl! — around to see it. He blinked rapidly.

The girl sighed and walked back toward him.

"It's scary I know, but you can't stay here. Bowltre will be back. And this time, Caleb might not be able to distract him."

"Who was that guy?" Grayson's voice came out as more of a squeak than he wanted.

"His name is Mr. Bowltre. He wants the wands. All of them. But he can't have them."

"Why not? If they're his, we could just give them back!"

"They're not his. They never were. Listen, we really have to go." Her voice grew higher pitched. "Can't you just trust me?"

Grayson really looked at her for the first time, forgetting his own fear for a moment. She was speaking to him very calmly, but her eyes kept flickering toward the deeper forest where that Bowltre guy had disappeared. There was sweat glistening on her forehead, and Grayson didn't think it was just from the heat of the day.

She was scared, too, he suddenly realized, but she was still taking the time to try to talk to him.

More importantly, he got a good feeling from this girl. She was safe. She wasn't out to hurt him, like he knew Bowltre had been.

Still, going with someone he didn't know…

Reluctantly, he nodded.

"Good," she said. "Now hurry."

She raced ahead of him, pushing out of the woods and back onto the baseball diamond. She didn't stop there, though. Instead, she ran straight across and back to the street. Once there, she led him down the block, back in the direction of Grayson's new house.

"She's taking me home," he thought, as he pounded along behind her.

Relief flooded through him. Just a short time ago he had been complaining that there was nothing to do. Now, he just wanted to get back inside, go to his room, shut the blinds, and play videogames. Maybe for the rest of his life.

But the girl didn't lead him home, after all. She veered off and ran between two houses. Grayson hesitated for a moment. His house wasn't that far away! Surely he could make it there safely.

Then, he remembered the bolts of lightning shooting from Bowltre's wand. Grayson could run reasonably fast, but there was no way he could outrun that.

Besides, when he thought about going home, he got a slight headache and his stomach cramped. When he turned back toward the girl, running farther ahead of him now, those bad feelings went away.

It was almost like something was telling him it wasn't safe to go home. Maybe he'd be leading Mr. Bowltre directly to Mom and Dad.

He shuddered and then began to run as fast as he could, trying to catch up to the girl.

When he came out from between the two houses, there was a fence on one side of him and someone else's driveway on the other. No one came to the door to yell at him for trespassing, though, and a moment later, he was out onto another street.

He looked around wildly, sure that he had lost the girl when he caught sight of her as she darted between another two houses farther down this new street.

It was all Grayson could do to keep up with her as she took first one passage between houses after another. Grayson felt like he was running forever, and soon he was panting for breath and had no idea where he was.

Finally, the girl slowed down. She ran into a yard and bent over with her hands on her knees. Grayson was glad to see that she was breathing heavily, as well.

"We're safe now," she managed to say. "At least, we will be in a minute."

She stood up and let out her breath in a giant whoosh.

"You run pretty fast," she told him.

"Thanks. So do you." He didn't say that she had almost lost him several times.

"I'm Sophia," the girl said, holding out her hand, just like an adult.

Grayson shook it, feeling that something important was happening. "I'm Grayson."

"Good. Now we're friends. I'll show you to our clubhouse in just a minute, but I want to wait for Caleb first."

"Who's Caleb?" He remembered her mentioning him in the woods.

Grayson wondered if all the kids around there were part of this club.

"He's kind of like the leader," Sophia said. "It's not like we *have* to wait for him. He can take care of himself, but I just want to— oh, there he is!"

A tall, lanky boy with dark skin was walking casually down the street toward them. He was dressed in jeans and a t-shirt like Sophia but was coming from a different direction than she had taken. His lips were pursed as he whistled quietly, and he was casually tossing something up and catching it again.

Whatever it was spun in the air, until Caleb caught it, holding it for the briefest of seconds before sending it spinning again.

In that brief moment, however, Grayson realized that Caleb had yet another wand.

Chapter 5

"Who's this?" Caleb asked easily as he stepped into the yard. He glanced at Grayson but spoke to Sophia.

"His name's Grayson," she said. "He's one of us now."

Caleb raised his eyebrows and turned to Grayson. "Huh. You found one. I didn't think there were any more. Let me see it."

Grayson held up the wand he'd found buried in the dirt.

Caleb peered at it but didn't try to take it. "No obvious marks," he said. "Do you know what it does?"

Grayson shook his head.

In truth, he was a little intimidated by Caleb. The other boy was quite a bit taller than he was and the way he'd sauntered down the street— whistling and playing catch with his wand— right after confronting Mr. Bowltre, told Grayson that Caleb had more confidence than he ever would.

"We'll find out." Caleb stuck out his hand, just like Sophia had. "I'm Caleb."

"Grayson," Grayson said as he took the offered hand.

He felt stupid. Sophia had already told Caleb his name. He dropped his eyes and braced for the laughter that was sure to follow.

When it didn't, Grayson looked up. Caleb wasn't laughing, but he was smiling. It was an easy smile, too. A friendly smile. One that said, "yeah, I know, but it's cool that you told me anyway." Grayson found himself responding to it.

"Thanks for the help," he said. "Both of you. That Bowltre guy was…"

"Scary, right?" Caleb hunched forward and opened his eyes wide. "I'm going to eat your face." He pitched his voice as deep as he could, which in no way sounded like Bowltre, but Grayson laughed anyway.

In truth, he had been going to say that Bowltre was terrifying, horrible, nightmarish, and any words like that he could think of. Scary didn't quite seem to do him justice.

"Scary. Yeah." He grinned, instead.

Caleb grew more serious. "He really is bad news. We do everything we can to stay away from him." He turned to Sophia. "Show him the clubhouse, yet?"

"No, we just got here," she replied.

"Slowpokes," he said, but again, it was with such an easy manner that Grayson didn't take offense.

He liked Caleb. And Sophia. Both of them were really cool. He'd only just met them, but something told him they were going to be great friends.

"Let's go then," Caleb said.

Sophia nodded and walked toward the back of the house. For a moment, Grayson thought she was leading them inside and that she must live there.

Instead of going to the door, however, she stopped near a section of the house that was just blank wall, with no windows or doors. The blue siding came down to a block foundation, and then the lawn started below that. Maybe she was just putting Grayson on?

Sophia pulled a wand out of her shirt. It was tied around her neck by a stout, leather cord that passed through a hole in the handle. She lifted it over her head and pointed it toward the foundation of the house.

"Reveality!" she commanded.

Suddenly, a door was there. It was like one of those old cellar doors Grayson had seen in movies, where the entrance to a— usually creepy— cellar was outside the house. Two large doors were designed to open from the middle.

Grayson couldn't believe his eyes. It was one thing to see Bowltre shoot lightning from a wand when he was in the middle of being scared to death, but it was quite another to see a door magically appear from nowhere in someone's yard on a bright, sunny day.

Caleb and Sophia both took it in stride, though. Sophia tucked her wand back into her shirt, while Caleb stuck his in his back pocket. They both grabbed a door and pulled.

Stairs led down. From where Grayson stood, he couldn't tell to what.

Without another word, Sophia ran down the steps and disappeared. Caleb turned back to Grayson.

"Come on. You first, then I'll shut the doors."

Grayson hesitated. This all seemed crazy; everything since he had tripped over that wand.

He looked down at it, still clenched tightly in his left fist. He hadn't let go of it since he'd first found it.

He looked back at Caleb and the stairs. His stomach stayed calm. Not like when he had thought of going home.

Slowly, he walked forward and peered down the steps. At the bottom was a concrete floor. It looked like there were lights on somewhere, maybe in the actual basement.

He was being silly. The stairs led to the basement of Sophia's house. They were just hidden by magic. What was so weird about that?

He stepped past Caleb and onto the stairs. A few seconds later, the doors behind him closed with a bang.

Chapter 6

The large room that he found himself in certainly looked like a basement. Except there was no washer or dryer, there was no furnace, or anything else he would have expected to see.

Instead, it was just an open room. Two old couches with ripped and stained cushions were at right-angles to each other, and there was another raggedy chair nearby. An old rug covered the cement floor and a low cabinet with one leg taped together was against another wall. A stained and dented refrigerator hummed quietly in the far corner.

But what really caught Grayson's eye was the bookshelf. Out of all the furniture in the room, it was the only thing that looked well taken care of. The wood was shiny and whole, and the shelves didn't even sag under the weight of several books.

Grayson loved to read. He did it almost every night when he went to bed, and he usually had a book on him when he was in between classes in school. So, as Sophia plopped down on one of the couches and Caleb went to the refrigerator, Grayson headed for the books.

He recognized a few of the titles. Some he had read; others he wanted to.

But there were several books that he'd never even heard of. Most looked old and well-used.

One, standing upright on its own shelf, between two bookends, caught his eye.

"The *Lost* Wands," he read aloud. "What's this?"

"It's a history," Caleb said.

"Or maybe an instruction manual," Sophia added.

"Or, it could be a warning," Caleb continued. "Do you want a soda?"

As soon as he asked, Grayson realized that his mouth and throat were very dry from all the running. "Yes, please," he said.

Caleb turned around with three cans of Coke. He tossed one to Sophia, who caught it expertly in one hand, and the other to Grayson, who fumbled with it before getting control.

"Careful opening that one now," Caleb grinned.

He moved to the other couch and sprawled onto it, his longs legs stretched out and one arm slung over the back.

Grayson stuck his wand into his back pocket, like Caleb carried his, and cracked his can slightly to let some of the gas out, then put his mouth over the hole and opened it a little farther. Cold soda sprayed out, but he swallowed as fast as he could until it stopped. When he looked up, he had to blink away tears the sharp, fizziness had caused.

"Nice one!" Sophia laughed. "I thought for sure you'd drench yourself!"

Grayson grinned and sat in the old chair, taking his time with his next sip. Then, he looked around the room.

"What is this place?" he asked.

"Wand Chaser headquarters," Caleb said. "It's where we come to relax and plan."

"Plan what?"

Caleb and Sophia looked at each other, then Caleb sat up and leaned forward. He reached back, brought his wand out, and gazed down at it

"This is Breaker," he finally said. "I've had it for over a year now."

"And this," Sophia pulled hers from her shirt and let it dangle from the cord, "is Sight-Blinder."

Grayson pulled his own wand back out of his pocket. "What's this one called?"

"That's up to you to decide," Caleb said. "You can call it whatever you want. Most of us name them for something that they do."

"Except Jonah," Sophia giggled.

"Yeah." Caleb grinned and rolled his eyes. "Jonah named his Pete. Just Pete."

Grayson felt like his head was spinning. There was too much happening, too fast. Who was Jonah? Were Caleb and Sophia saying there were more kids around? And that they all had wands? And what had Caleb called this place? The Wand Chaser headquarters or something?

"It's okay," Caleb said. "It's a lot, I know. We all went through it."

"I just... I mean, we just moved here. Me and my parents. I was just trying to find someone to play baseball with."

Caleb and Sophia looked at each other again, but Grayson noticed that this time they seemed more...sad.

"Yeah," Sophia said. "There's probably not too much chance of that happening."

"Because of the wands?" Grayson asked. "That doesn't seem right. We could just leave them alone for a bit and—"

But Caleb was shaking his head. "Not because of the wands. Or not *just* because of them. It's because we're too busy. We have work to do. It's important and there's no one else who can do it."

"What about your parents?" Grayson asked.

He had never been one of those kids who wanted to grow up too fast. He was happy letting his Mom and Dad solve problems. It gave him more time to do the things he wanted to do. So, why not let their parents deal with these wands and he and his new friends— and they did feel like friends— could play ball, or ride bikes, or play video games, or whatever they wanted? It was summer, after all. They had to make the most of it.

"That's a problem," Sophia said. "Our parents can't do it."

"Why not?"

"Because they don't remember us," she shrugged.

"And soon," Caleb added, "yours won't remember *you*, either."

Chapter 7

Grayson paused with the can of Coke halfway to his mouth. He stared at Caleb for a moment, then lowered his soda without taking a drink and started to laugh.

"Good one," he said. "You got me."

But Caleb wasn't laughing. Neither was Sophia. Both of them were just watching him, waiting for him to see that they weren't joking.

A cold wind seemed to blow right through Grayson's guts.

"What are you talking about?" he whispered.

"It's true." Sophia sounded like she could have been talking about the weather. "They don't see or remember us at all. No one does."

"That can't be true," Grayson protested.

"I know it's a lot to swallow—"

Grayson leapt to his feet, cutting off whatever Caleb had been about to say.

"It's not true!" he shouted.

He ran to the stairs, ignoring Caleb's cry of "wait!" from behind him. He hit the doors at the

top as hard as he could and they flew open.
Grayson ran across the yard and back to the street.

As he sped away, he glanced back, but the doors
to the Wand Chaser's clubhouse had disappeared.

He ran back the way he had come when
following Sophia, ducking between houses. Or at
least, he thought it was the way he had come. After
a few minutes, he realized that all the houses looked
similar, and he hadn't been paying much attention
before. He'd been too busy chasing after her.

He slowed down and tried to get his bearings.

It was then that he noticed his stomach was
hurting.

He didn't care! He was going home and he'd
spend the rest of his summer doing his own thing.
Let those other stupid kids play their weird games
without him.

By now, Grayson had half-convinced himself
that it *was* all some sort of game. A way of ragging
on the new guy.

But what about Mr. Bowltre and the lightning
that came out of his wand?

A small, persistent voice kept asking him that
question, over and over as he tried to find his way
home.

Grayson passed between two houses again,
setting off a dog barking inside and came out onto a
street that he thought might be his own. He looked

to the right, but wasn't sure he recognized anything, and then to his left. He didn't see much difference.

"To the right then," he decided and started in that direction.

Before he'd gone more than a few paces, an eerie, cold sensation came over him. It was like when he first saw Mr. Bowltre. Hide, it said. Hide and stay quiet.

Grayson looked around, but there wasn't any place to go. There were just houses, with garages that were shut and fences along most of the backyards. Cars were in some of the driveways, but that wasn't going to be good enough.

Hide!

The urge was even stronger now. Grayson almost whimpered with the need to get out of sight.

There! A tree, bigger than most stood in the corner of a yard three houses away. Grayson ran as fast as he could, leapt, and grabbed the lower branches.

Hurry! Hide!

He scrambled up almost as far as he dared to go.

Stomp, drag. Stomp, drag.

Mr. Bowltre was coming! He was on the sidewalk, heading in Grayson's direction. This time, there was no Sophia to hide him.

Grayson slowly— very slowly— reached up to the next branch, the topmost one he'd trust to support his weight. He pulled himself up, using his legs around the trunk to try to stop from shaking the tree too much and giving his hiding place away.

Stomp, drag.

He was still coming.

Grayson stopped moving entirely, his arms wrapped around a branch and his legs still encircling the trunk. It wasn't a very good position to be stuck in, but Bowltre was now too near to risk moving.

Stomp, drag. Stomp, drag. Stomp… stop.

Grayson didn't dare look down. If he did, he knew he would see Bowltre staring up at him with those horrible, protruding eyes and crazy, spiked hair. He'd lick his lips and open his mouth and tell him to "come down, boy" and Grayson would have no choice.

His arms trembled from both fear and the strain of holding himself up.

"Where are you, boy?" Bowltre's voice rumbled up to him. "I can smell you. Thief. Wicked boy."

Grayson heard Bowltre sniff again. "You're near. So close."

Everything went silent. Grayson shut his eyes and prayed that Mr. Bowltre would just go away and that he could go home.

Stomp, drag.

"I'll find you, boy. Then, I'll punish you and punish you."

Stomp, drag.

Mr. Bowltre took another step away. Grayson almost let himself down to the branch he had been standing on, but some inner voice told him not yet. So he stayed where he was, his arms and legs cramping up so badly he thought he'd never be able to move.

There was a dog-like growl of frustration as Mr. Bowltre moved away. The sound of his unusual gait began to fade, but Grayson still refused to move. What if it was a trick? What if Bowltre was just pretending to move, but was only taking lighter steps? What if he was still there, staring and searching?

Finally, it didn't matter. Grayson's arms gave out and slipped from the branch he'd been holding onto.

He tried to catch his balance, but no such luck. His feet slipped too, and before he knew it, he was tumbling through the tree, trying to grab any branch he could to slow his fall. His breath slammed out of him in a strangled wheeze when he crashed to the foot of the tree. It felt like he would never breathe again, and his whole body hurt. For a moment, he forgot all about Bowltre.

Then, the memory of the horrible man standing right underneath him returned, and Grayson sat up with a gasp.

Mr. Bowltre was nowhere to be seen.

Where he went, Grayson didn't know, but he was sure the man was gone. He could just feel it.

He staggered to his feet, drew in a raggedy breath, and began again to try to find his way home.

Chapter 8

Grayson recognized the street. His house was only a short distance away.

During the rest of his walk, he hadn't felt that urge to hide, so he knew that Bowltre wasn't around. But the closer he got to home, the more his stomach hurt, until it felt like he had a pair of sharp scissors poking him from the inside out.

He ignored it as best he could, ran the final few yards, and burst inside.

"Mom? Dad? I'm home!"

When he shut the door behind him, he sagged against it. A rush of relief washed over him so strongly that he thought he might start crying. But he held it together, crossed his arms over his aching stomach, and went to find his parents.

It had been early afternoon when he'd left the house, and he hadn't realized how much time had passed until he'd come out of the Wand Chasers clubhouse and saw that the sun was beginning to go down. Now, between hiding from Mr. Bowltre and having to find his way, it was almost dark and probably past dinner.

Mom was going to be very angry.

"Sorry I'm late," he called. He pushed himself away from the door and started toward the kitchen. The smell of pizza wafted out to him, but it only seemed to make the ache in his stomach that much worse.

His parents weren't in the kitchen. If there had been pizza, it was either gone, or the leftovers had already been picked up and put in the fridge.

"Mom?"

No one answered him, but Grayson heard the noise of the television from the living room. When he'd left earlier, it hadn't even been hooked up yet, but his Dad must have gotten it done when he came home from his new job.

Grayson supposed that was a good thing, especially since he planned on being inside for most of the summer now.

Both of his parents were in the living room. His dad was on the sofa, and his mother was going through unpacked boxes and paying half-attention to the program on the TV. His father was starting to doze off already.

"Sorry I'm late, Mom," Grayson said again.

His mother didn't respond for a moment, then she looked at him. She frowned for a moment, and

Grayson's stomach flipped over, but then she smiled.

"Hi, Honey," she said. "I'm sorry, I didn't hear you come in."

His father never even stirred.

"It's okay," Grayson replied. "I just go home. I was…"

His mother had gone back to what she was doing and watching the television.

"Mom?" He tried again. "Was there pizza?"

"What?" She turned back to him, and again, he saw that brief flicker of a frown. "Oh, hi Honey. Just get home?"

"Yeah, I just said that. I wanted to know—"

She turned away, right in the middle of his question, without bothering to answer it at all.

"Dad?" he tried.

But his father only started to snore louder, which caused his mother to scowl and pick up the remote to turn the TV louder.

"I guess I'll just go to my room, then," Grayson said.

He might as well have been talking to himself.

"Night," he said.

No one answered him.

His steps were heavy as he made his way down the unfamiliar hallway to his new, strange bedroom.

Once there, he turned the light on and looked around.

All of his stuff was still in boxes. Most were toys and games. Several were his books, which were supposed to go on a new shelf that Dad had promised he would put up. A few were labeled in his mom's neat handwriting and said things like, "Grayson clothes-closet," or "Grayson clothes-dresser."

His bed was still unmade. The frame hadn't even been put together. It lay on the floor in a pile with his mattress and box-spring leaning against the wall. Grayson moved the rails and some boxes until he had made room and pulled the mattress down so that he could lie on it. He found a box labeled "Grayson's bed" and took out a sheet and blanket and then found his pillow.

It was still pretty early, but he was tired. More tired than he could ever remember being. And his stomach still hurt. He thought of the pizza that he'd missed out on. Instead of making him hungry, it only made him feel sick.

He laid down on the mattress and curled up, trying to ignore the sound of the television from the other room. Eventually, his eyes closed, and he fell asleep.

When he woke up, it was dark. Someone had turned out his light.

Faintly, he heard a noise from outside. He bolted upright.

Stomp, drag. Stomp, drag.

It sounded like Bowltre was passing by the house, very slowly. Grayson could picture him, his head thrown back while he sniffed the air and his huge eyes searching.

Grayson lay back down and curled into a ball under his sheet. He squeezed his eyes shut, willing Mr. Bowltre to just go away.

It was a long time before he was able to fall asleep again.

Chapter 9

Things weren't any better when Grayson got up the next morning, except that now it was light outside and he'd be able to see if Mr. Bowltre was coming after him.

When he went out to the kitchen, his dad was already gone, and his mom didn't seem to notice him. Not even when he asked her what was for breakfast. So he got himself a bowl of cold cereal and ate it at the table by himself, while his mom unpacked more dishes.

It occurred to him that before he had found the wand, his mother had been acting completely normal. She was the one who suggested that he go out yesterday and make some new friends. She'd kissed the top of his head and told him that she loved him before he left.

Now, he might as well not even be there. Twice while he was eating, she put something on the table near him but never once even spoke to him.

When he finished eating, he rinsed out his bowl, put it in the sink, and returned to his room. There wasn't much to do there. He wasn't in the mood to read, his video game wasn't hooked up yet, and he didn't feel like doing that, anyway. So he sat on his mattress and thought.

The wand he'd found yesterday had spent the night under his pillow, and it was the first thing he'd touched when he woke up. He'd put it in the back pocket of his jeans before he went out to the kitchen. But he didn't have it yesterday.

Maybe that was the answer! Having the wand with him was what was causing his mother to act so strangely!

He set the wand down on his dresser and left his bedroom.

His stomach felt funny, like he was doing something wrong. Then again, his stomach had been a little upset the whole time since he'd left the Wand Chasers clubhouse.

"Hey, Mom!" he called.

His mother still didn't answer, although he could hear her moving around, unpacking more boxes.

Grayson went back into the living room where she was working now.

"Mom?"

His mother paused for a second, like she thought she heard something, but then shrugged and kept on working.

Grayson stood in front of her. "Mom!"

His voice broke and tears started to form in his eyes.

Maybe Bowltre had killed him and he was a ghost. His mother didn't even pause at his yell. Instead, she just moved around Grayson without even glancing at him. It was like he was invisible.

Shoulders slumped, he returned to his room and picked up the wand. His stomach felt slightly better, but it still wasn't normal.

"I hate you," he whispered, looking down at it. "This is all your fault."

He didn't know if that was true or not. Maybe just being in this stupid town was enough to make his mom and dad forget him. Or maybe it was something Mr. Bowltre was doing. All Grayson knew was that none of it had happened until he'd found the wand.

"I ought to throw you away," he said. "Or break you."

He grabbed the pointed end with his other hand and tried to bend it. The wand flexed a small amount, but that was all. Grayson hadn't actually thought he'd be able to break it and wasn't even sure he really wanted to.

It turned out that it didn't matter what he wanted. The wand didn't even come close to snapping.

In a way, Grayson was glad.

Things were horrible, and he was sad and confused. And he was angry, but even more, he was scared.

Somehow, though, knowing that he had the wand made him feel a little bit better. If only he knew what it did.

He had no idea how to go about trying to make it work.

If he wanted to find *that* out, there was only one place to go.

Chapter 10

The doors leading to the clubhouse weren't visible when Grayson found his way back to them.

He'd walked slowly, staying alert for any sign of Bowltre and allowed his "feelings" to guide him. He discovered that if he just sort-of listened, he knew which way to go.

Once, he thought he heard the stomp, drag of Mr. Bowltre's footsteps, but it was pretty far away, and he never got the urge to hide. Instead, he crossed from one street to another, and soon, he was back at the clubhouse.

But now, he had no idea how to get inside. He assumed that the house was where Sophia lived, but he didn't really know that. And, even if she did, would anyone answer the door if he knocked? Would they even see him, or know who Sophia was?

He didn't think it was likely and, truthfully, the thought of being ignored like that again was too much.

Instead, he attempted to find the cellar door on his own. He walked to where he remembered them being and put out a foot, trying to find it that way. There was nothing different. His foot came down on the grass, and Grayson walked all the way to the wall of the house. He tried to touch it with his hand, and even, on an impulse, with his wand, but nothing worked.

The door simply wasn't there.

So, he sat next to the house, in the shade, and waited.

The sun was warm already and there wasn't much noise in the neighborhood, which seemed odd. Soon, Grayson started to nod off.

"Hey!"

He woke to the sound of Sophia's amused greeting.

"Why are you sitting on the doors?"

Grayson blinked at her and then looked around. "I'm not. I'm sitting on the ground."

Sophia grinned and flourished her wand. "Nope. On the doors," she said. "Reveality!"

Grayson *was* sitting on the doors. He was on the highest end of the slanting structure so that he was a couple of feet higher than the ground.

"I don't understand," he said. "Why couldn't I feel them?"

"Because of Sight-blinder," she replied happily. "Come on, and I'll explain."

Grayson helped her open the doors and followed her into the basement clubhouse, where Sophia pulled a jug of orange juice from the refrigerator and took a big swig. She offered it to Grayson, who did the same.

"I love orange juice," Sophia said.

"Me, too," Grayson replied. He hesitated, but then asked. "Can you please tell me what's going on?"

"Sure. Let's sit down. Caleb will be here soon, and probably one or two others. Do you want to wait? He knows more than I do."

"Can you at least tell me some?" Grayson asked. "I'm really… I…"

"I know." Sophia looked at him kindly. "I'm one of the newer ones, too. My parents just moved here a couple of months ago, so I remember how it feels." She glanced at the ceiling, which was the floor of the house overhead. "I miss my mom."

Then, she sighed and shrugged her shoulders. "But that's why we're so busy. Right?"

She grinned and flopped onto a couch. "Ask away!"

Grayson sank more slowly into the same chair he'd sat in the day before. He was trying to think of all the things he wanted to ask. Why? How? And each of those questions relating to so many things. Finally, he settled on one question that seemed easiest to ask.

"Why couldn't I feel the doors? If your wand is Sight-blinder, I shouldn't be able to *see* something, but I should still be able to *feel* it."

"That's just its name. The one I gave it. Because it sounded better than 'everything-blinder' or something. My wand can hide anything, and then it can't be seen, heard, or felt."

Grayson thought back. "Is that how we hid from Mr. Bowltre yesterday?"

"Yep!" Sophia grinned. "But he's tricky. I never thought about smell, and I'm not sure if my wand hides that. He might have been bluffing. Still, I was glad Caleb lured him away."

Grayson was too, because he was pretty sure that Bowltre had gotten his scent, all right.

"In the tree, too," Sophia said quietly.

That got Grayson's attention back on her. "What tree?"

"The one you climbed. We followed you. We wanted to make sure you were safe. When you climbed the tree, I used Sight-blinder to hide you."

"Oh. Then, you saw me fall?"

Sophia tried to hide her grin. "Yeah, and then we stuck around to make sure you were okay. When you got home—"

"We knew you'd be safe." Caleb came down the stairs. "We also knew that it was the only way you were going to believe us."

Grayson wasn't sure how he felt about that. On the one hand, he was glad that his new friends had cared enough to follow and watch out for him. On the other, he was pretty embarrassed by his behavior.

"I'm sorry for—"

"Forget it," Caleb said. "We get it. I wouldn't have believed us, either. Now we just need to move on."

"Okay." Grayson took a deep breath and stood up. "I'm ready. For whatever is next."

Caleb smiled. "All right!"

Sophia jumped to her feet, spit in her palm, and held her hand out. Grayson spit in his own and clasped hers, then Caleb's own spit-moistened hand.

"What's next?" he asked.

Caleb and Sophia looked at each other, then turned back to Grayson and, in one voice, said, "Adam."

Chapter 11

"Adam? What's that supposed to mean?" Grayson asked.

"Not what. Who." Caleb paused to think. "He's… well, really, you have to meet him. Then you'll understand. I guess you could think of him like our club adviser, though."

"That's one thing to call him," a new voice said.

The boy who came down the stairs and into the clubhouse was shorter than Grayson, but bigger around. He wore glasses and had thick black hair parted on the side. In his hands he held another wand, and he was smiling cheerfully.

"Hi! I'm Jonah! And this is Pete!"

He held the wand out in one hand and waved his other up and down next to it, like he was demonstrating some amazing product on a television ad.

"Um. I'm Grayson." He took his wand out of his back pocket. Maybe this was how the kids here talked? "And this is… umm… I don't know…"

Jonah laughed. "Because you don't know what it does, right? Ha! Don't let these two make you think you have to wait. I named mine Pete before I knew what it did. Is there any orange juice left? Or did Sam not make anymore?"

Jonah spoke with a fast-paced energy that was a bit hard to keep up with. Before Grayson even had a chance to answer anything, the other boy had moved to the refrigerator and opened it. He was now gulping down orange juice in huge swallows.

"Sam makes orange juice?" Grayson asked weakly. It was the only thing that stuck with him from Jonah's quick speech.

"Not really," Caleb grinned. "Her wand just brings things to her. So she can ask it for OJ and it comes. We don't really know from where."

"Isn't that stealing?" Grayson asked.

Caleb shrugged. "Maybe. But no one remembers us or acknowledges us when we're right in front of them. Without Sam, we'd have a much harder time of it."

"Oh. Okay." Grayson guessed that made sense. At least, it made as much sense as anything else that had been happening to him these last two days. Then he thought back to his own parents. It hadn't even occurred to him until that moment, but they weren't going to take care of him. He was on his own now. Maybe forever.

Or at least until he could figure out how to make them remember him.

"You guys are going to Adam's?" Jonah asked. He let out a huge burp.

"I think that's best," Caleb said. "He'll be able to help Grayson. Like he did with most of us."

"Don't forget the book," Jonah said. "You know how he gets if you don't bring it." He made an angry face, then grinned and gulped more orange juice.

"Right, thanks for reminding me." Caleb pulled the book Grayson had noticed the day before, "*The Lost Wands*", off the shelf and tucked it under his arm. "All right. Ready?"

"I guess so," Grayson replied.

Caleb stepped closer to him.

"Don't be nervous," he said. "Adam is going to help. He's been trying to help us all."

Grayson shifted his weight from foot to foot. "I'm not nervous. I'm just…"

"Freaked out," Caleb grinned. "You're not the first."

Grayson grinned back. Caleb really did have a way of making things seem like they were going to be okay, somehow. He nodded. "Yeah. Freaked out is the right word."

"Two words, actually," Jonah said.

"Anyone coming with us?" Caleb asked.

"I will," Sophia said. "I want to ask Adam a few things anyway."

"Not me!" Jonah opened the rickety cabinet and pulled out a stack of tattered comic books. "I've got some literature to catch up on. Besides, that guy freaks *me* out."

Caleb dashed up the stairs and Grayson followed him. It wasn't until the three of them were walking down the street that Jonah's comment sunk in.

"What did he mean by Adam freaking him out?" he asked.

"Oh, that's just Jonah being Jonah," Sophia said. "He likes to be dramatic."

"Well, in fairness, Adam can be a bit of sight," Caleb said. "But I don't think that's why he said it."

Sophia didn't reply, so Grayson did instead. "Why, then?"

Caleb made sure the book was still secured under his arm before answering. "He probably gets nervous because Adam and Bowltre used to be best friends."

Chapter 12

Grayson didn't know how he was supposed to respond to what Caleb had just said.

What he did know was that ever since he'd left his house that morning and started back to the clubhouse, his stomach had felt better. It was something he was starting to trust more and more. Going to see Adam— whoever he was— didn't make him feel sick, so Grayson was fairly sure that it was the right thing to do.

Caleb and Sophia laughed and joked around. Grayson followed behind, not really taking part.

It wasn't that he felt excluded. He knew that if he stepped up and joined in the kidding it would be fine. It was more that he felt on edge, but not from his stomachache.

Mr. Bowltre was still out there. Sophia could hide them, if it became necessary, but Grayson thought Bowltre was onto something. He had definitely smelled Grayson yesterday, even though he couldn't see or hear him. Maybe he was learning another way to find something or someone that Sophia had hidden.

In which case, it would be much better to know that he was near, than to be surprised by him, so Grayson was staying on alert.

The other two just kept walking, a long way down the same street the clubhouse was on and then around the corner. Soon, the houses and the lots they sat on started getting larger.

"Guys?" Grayson asked. "How much farther?"

"Not much," Caleb said. "You can relax, you know? Bowltre wouldn't dare come to this neighborhood."

Grayson wasn't so sure of that. Something was beginning to prey on the edge of his mind. It was like the feeling he got in school when the teacher gave a quiz he hadn't studied for. Like something wasn't going to go well.

Stomp, drag.

Grayson stopped walking, but the other two continued.

He waited but didn't hear anything else. Maybe he'd been mistaken. He was thinking about it a lot and his mind was—

Stomp, drag.

No, he definitely heard it! Bowltre was near!

Ahead of him, Caleb and Sophia had noticed that he'd stopped and turned around.

"What are you doing?" Sophia asked. "We're almost there."

Grayson shook his head, feeling like his eyes were almost as wide as Bowltre's protruding ones. "He's here." His voice was a squeaky whisper.

Caleb pulled out his wand and looked around. "No. I don't see him. Where?"

Stomp, drag. Stomp, drag.

The sound of Bowltre's footsteps were much closer now. Close enough that he should be in plain sight.

Close enough that his friends now heard the footsteps, too.

"Where is he?" Sophia asked. She pulled out her wand, as well, but Grayson thought it was too late to hide them.

There was an ear-splitting crack as lightning flashed in a bolt that barely missed Caleb.

The taller boy dove to the side and rolled, moving more quickly than Grayson would have believed possible. He came back to his feet pointing his wand, but still couldn't see what to aim at.

"There!" Grayson pointed at an empty part of the street, not far from where he stood.

"There's nothing there!" Caleb yelled back.

Another bolt of lightning snapped into the air, this time actually hitting Sophia, who cried out and collapsed in a heap.

Grayson didn't know what Caleb's wand could do, but the fact that he called it Breaker must have meant something.

"There! There!" He pointed frantically.

"Quiet, boy," Bowltre's voice snarled. "When I'm through with them, we'll have a talk. We'll talk and then you'll give it to me. Then we'll decide your punishment."

"There!" Grayson screamed one more time.

Caleb grimaced, jabbed his wand at the ground where Grayson was pointing, and shouted. "Destructia!"

The ground jumped violently. Grayson stumbled, but not so much that he didn't see a huge crack suddenly appear in the street. It ran for several yards and was at least three feet wide.

A growled curse came from the air, and then Bowltre was visible as he tumbled into the crack in the street.

It was wide enough that he fell in, but it wasn't that deep. Grayson heard him hit the bottom immediately, and then Bowltre began muttering again.

"Close it!" Grayson yelled.

Let the crack close and crush Bowltre, he thought. Then they wouldn't have to worry about him anymore.

But even as he said it, a sharp pain flared in his stomach, strong enough to bend him double.

It wasn't the right thing to do, he realized. Not even to Bowltre. In fact, it was a horribly wrong thing to do.

"I can't," Caleb called. He was already pulling Sophia to her feet. "It's Breaker, not Fixer! Come on! Without Sophia, we need to get out of here!"

Grayson ran and grabbed Sophia's other arm, so that one of hers was over each of their shoulders. He and Caleb staggered down the sidewalk, dragging her along. Grayson glanced at his new friend's face, but she appeared to be sound asleep... at least.

"Is she...?"

"No," Caleb answered immediately, but Grayson didn't think he sounded sure. "Adam can help her."

Behind them, Grayson thought he heard the stomp, drag of Bowltre's footsteps. If he did, it was only once. He looked back, but the crack in the street was the only thing to be seen. If Bowltre had climbed out, he was either gone or had gone back to being invisible.

Grayson also couldn't help but notice that there had been lightning bolts firing down the streets, three kids screaming, and a sudden large split in the street, and yet, no one from any of the large, beautiful houses they staggered past seemed to care at all.

Chapter 13

Bowltre wasn't gone. Grayson suddenly felt his presence again, just as he'd felt the sudden urge to *hurry*.

He ran faster and Caleb kept pace with him. Between them, Sophia moaned.

Stomp, drag, stomp, drag, stomp, drag!

Left.

The feeling to run to the left was so strong it almost sounded like someone had shouted at him.

With no time to explain, Grayson veered that way, dragging both Sophia and Caleb with him. A lightning bolt streaked by, just missing them but exploding against a traffic sign with a horrendous crash.

"What are you doing?" Caleb yelled. "Adam's house is that way!" He used his free hand to point to the right.

"Trust me!" Grayson yelled back.

He let his wand and his gut guide him. He knew that the wand was doing it. If he let it, it spoke to him and told him what to—

Down.

Grayson ducked, pulling the other two with him.

More lightning flashed by overhead, shattering a tree limb.

Now.

"Now!" Grayson yelled. "Which house?"

"That one!"

Caleb ran toward a large, stone house with a lot of flowers and bushes in the front. A low, stone wall ran around the edge of the yard, with a closed, metal gate across the walkway.

Bowltre growled behind them, sounding more dog-like than ever.

"It's mine, boy! Mine! Thief! Wicked!"

Then, he howled, and the sound sent shivers down Grayson's spine.

"Let me go," Sophia suddenly said. "I can run myself!"

"You're hurt," Grayson protested, but Caleb let go of her right away.

Sophia punched Grayson in the shoulder.

"Hey!' But he let her go.

She staggered a little, but took off running, quickly catching Caleb.

Grayson glanced behind him and saw Mr. Bowltre closing the distance to him. He was flickering in and out of sight and running as fast as his limp would allow.

Stomp, drag! Stomp, drag!

Grayson ran faster.

Ahead of him, Sophia hit the gate, pushed it open, and tumbled through. Caleb hurdled the stone wall. A moment later, Grayson stumbled through the opening and fell next to Sophia.

He spun around on his knees, expecting Mr. Bowltre to follow.

The hunchbacked man stood panting, several yards away. Still on the street, he stared at them with his bugged-out eyes. Drool ran down his chin and he snarled.

Caleb raised Breaker and pointed it at him, but Bowltre only laughed. He held up his own wand, which wasn't the same that Grayson had seen in the woods yesterday. This one was a light, golden color.

"Go ahead, boy," he goaded. "Use your wand."

Caleb didn't lower his wand, but he didn't use it either. Instead, he smiled at Bowltre. "Go home. You can't come in here and you know it."

Bowltre drew himself up as straight as he could and glared at them. When he spoke, his voice was almost normal.

"You'll have to leave eventually. I'll be waiting."

Without another word, he turned and walked away. Stomp, drag. Stomp, drag.

Grayson let himself flop back onto the grass and tried to catch his breath. Caleb plopped down next to him and Sophia sat with her back against the wall. All three were still breathing heavily, and Sophia kept rubbing at her temples.

"Why aren't you more hurt?" Grayson finally asked.

"The lightning only grazed me; I think. Or maybe... I don't know." She shrugged. "Maybe it's not real lightning?"

"Or maybe you're just that tough," Caleb grinned.

Grayson pushed himself up and looked at the house. Made of gray stone and two stories high, it had a round sort-of tower at one corner with a pointed roof. A ramp led from the walkway to the front door.

Caleb saw him looking. "Adam's house. We're safe here. Mr. Bowltre can't come on this property, literally"

Sophia climbed to her feet. "Come on. He's waiting for us."

In the downstairs window of the tower, a man was watching them. He noticed Grayson and nodded once, but he didn't look happy to see him.

Chapter 14

The first thing Grayson noticed was how gloomy the house was on the inside. Everything was made of heavy dark wood and thick curtains covered most of the windows. There were books and various other items covering every flat surface. Some of the books looked pretty cool, if Grayson had the time to check them out, but he didn't.

"In here," a voice called, as they entered the main hall.

The voice came out of a wide doorway to their right. On the left, a stairway ran to a second floor, but the lower steps were covered with so many books and stacks of things that they couldn't have really been used.

"Hurry up, now," the voice urged. "We've got a lot to discuss."

Even in the dark, crowded house, the voice was pleasant. It contained none of the dog-like gruffness of Mr. Bowltre's, and, more importantly, it was the voice of an adult who was actually speaking to them.

Grayson followed his friends into the room. It was much brighter than the hallway had been, mostly because of three large windows set into the curving wall. They were in the downstairs room of the short tower Grayson had noticed on the outside.

But it was the man in the center of the room who caught Grayson's attention.

Adam, if that's who it was, sat in a wheelchair, with a blanket on his lap that hid his legs from view. He had brown hair, with some gray sparkling in it, and a pleasant face that regarded Grayson with soft, brown eyes.

He smiled, but the expression never seemed to reach those eyes.

"Hi," the man said. "My name is Adam. I'm sorry you got involved with all of this. It's not fair to you."

Ah. Grayson understood. The man hadn't looked out the window like that because he didn't like Grayson, he just didn't want to see another kid tied up with the wands.

"I'm Grayson," he said. "Thanks for… umm."

He really wasn't sure what he was thanking Adam for. Other than letting them walk in the door, he hadn't done anything.

Adam seemed to understand.

"Do you want something to drink?" he asked. "Caleb, can you get some water for everyone? I'll take some, too, if you don't mind. Oh, and leave the book, please."

"Sure," Caleb said. He handed Adam the book, who put it on his lap. He patted Grayson on the shoulder as he left.

Adam turned his gaze to Sophia.

"Could you help him, please?"

"Help him? With getting water?" Then she stopped and looked at Grayson out of the corner of her eye. "Oh! Sure. Help. Yep. I'll help with the water. Tricky stuff, that water…"

She kept rambling as she also left the room, leaving Grayson alone with the man.

Adam moved back a little and waved an arm toward a chair. "Sit down if you want," he said. "You can just move that stuff wherever."

The chair he'd indicated had a stack of several books occupying it, but it only took Grayson a moment to move them and take a seat.

Adam continued to stare at him for a moment, and then said. "Has it started happening yet?"

"What?" Grayson asked.

"With your parents. Have they…?"

"Oh, that. Yeah." Grayson cleared his throat, trying to swallow the sudden lump in it. "Yeah. Mom kind of remembered me last night, but Dad didn't at all. It was like I wasn't even there. This morning, Mom didn't either."

Adam nodded. "It goes fast. I'm sorry for that, but we are going to try to fix it. It's why I formed the Wand Chasers Club."

"Caleb and Sophia said something like that."

"They're good," Adam said. "The best in the club, really. And their wands can do a lot. They just have to learn to use them better. All of you do, really. Do you have yours?"

Grayson pulled it from his back pocket and held it out.

Adam pushed his wheelchair closer and gently took it. He examined it closely, holding it up and turning it so that he could peer at it from every side.

"Hmmm," he murmured. "I don't think I know this one."

He handed the wand back to Grayson and opened the book on his lap. He rapidly flipped through the pages, muttering to himself every now and then.

"Ah!" he finally exclaimed. "I think I have something!"

He picked up the book to show Grayson what he had found, and when he did he accidentally grabbed his lap-blanket as well. It came loose and fell to the floor.

Grayson started to bend down to collect it for the man but froze when he saw Adam's legs.

Chapter 15

Adam's legs were wood. Not like the pictures in a book of a pirate with a peg-leg. And not shaped to look like a leg made of flesh and bone. Adam's legs looked like thick, old stumps, with gnarled bark that stuck up in places. He wore pants that had been cut-off above the knees. From there, Adams legs turned to wood from below the knees to where his feet should be, where they just sort of ended.

Grayson gasped and quickly sat back. He darted a look at Adam, but the man only smiled gently.

"It's okay," he said. "I was going to tell you anyway."

Grayson swallowed hard. "What happened?"

It was rude to ask such a thing, and his mother wouldn't have been happy to hear him do it, but he felt like he had to know.

Adam didn't seem to mind.

"I kept a wand too long," he answered. "They're not for adults."

"And it… it did that?"

"It did. Well, something did. My wand didn't turn things to wood. It kept people safe, sort of like Sophia's. Only mine could create a safe space, where only those I wanted to could enter. Over the years, I got stronger and could make that space larger and last longer."

"Like your house," Grayson said. "That's why Mr. Bowltre can't come here but we could." He stopped, the implication of what he was saying sinking in. "But that means…"

"Yes," Adam said. "I still have it, and I'm still using it. All the time. And all the time, this—" He reached down and rapped his knuckles on the wood that was his legs, "— goes a little bit higher and higher. Soon, I imagine, I won't be able to bend my legs, and then I'll have to figure something else out."

"But why?" Grayson asked. "Why don't you just get rid of it?"

"Then we wouldn't have any safe place," Caleb said. He'd re-entered the room holding two glasses of water, followed by Sophia who carried two more.

"But, what about the clubhouse?" Grayson thought he already knew the answer.

"That's just hidden," Sophia said. "If Bowltre ever finds it, he can get into it. Not like here."

Grayson turned back to Adam. "If Mr. Bowltre was gone, then you could stop using the wand. Would your legs go back to normal?"

"I don't know," Adam answered. "This is the only book I know of that talks about the wands, and I've never read anything about this."

He frowned down at the large book that still lay open on his lap. His face brightened. "But I did find something!" He turned the book so that Grayson could see the drawing. "Look familiar?"

The illustration did look like Grayson's wand. It might have been a little different at the handle, but that could have been just because of the drawing.

"It's my wand," he said. "What does it say?"

The language of the book was English but written in such elaborate characters that Grayson had a hard time making it out.

"It says that this is a wand of finding," Adam said. He turned the book around to face him again. "It's rare. One of the more rare ones I've heard of, as a matter of fact."

"So what does it do?" Sophia asked. "Anything cool?"

Adam read silently for a moment, then shrugged. "It doesn't say much. Just that this wand can help its bearer find a way. That's really all."

"Pfft." Sophia scoffed. "That's dumb. Almost as dumb as Jonah's Pete."

"It's not dumb," Grayson said. He was staring down at the wand, which he held loosely in his hand. "It saved us on the way here."

He looked up and told the other three what had happened while Bowltre was chasing them and how he was able to avoid his lightning blasts.

"Grayson," Adam said slowly. "Are you telling me that your wand actually spoke to you? That would be… very… unusual."

"No," Grayson replied. "It didn't speak to me exactly. Not with words. It was more like a really strong feeling that we should go left, and then duck down, and then run here as fast as we could. That's all."

"That's enough," Adam muttered. He stared at Grayson's wand. "I wonder what else it can tell you?"

Adam already had an idea, but Caleb spoke up first. "Ask it how to get rid of Bowltre."

"Uh-uh," Sophia said. "Ask it how to fix Adam's legs!"

But neither of those things was what Grayson wanted to ask his wand.

"No," he said quietly. "First, I want to ask how to make my Mom and Dad remember me."

Chapter 16

"That's a good start," Adam agreed. "And a fine use of the wand, if you ask me. If you can figure that out, you can do the same for Caleb and Sophia, and then all the rest of the kids."

He closed the book, while Caleb and Sophia sat forward, their eyes intent on Grayson, waiting for him to proceed.

The problem, Grayson realized as he gazed down at his wand, was that he had no idea *how* to do it. He didn't know how to make his wand work. So far, it had just sort of told him what was needed at the moment. He hadn't asked it for anything.

"Umm… hello?" he tried.

The wand didn't answer him.

"Hello?" He tried again. "Can you hear me?"

"It's a wand, not a cell-phone!" Sophia said. "You have to tell it what to do. Like this!"

She pointed her wand at the glass of water Grayson held and said, "Invisio!"

Grayson could still feel the cool glass in his hand, but there was no visible sign of it.

"Or like this," Caleb said. He pointed his wand at Grayson's hand, but Adam stopped him.

"I like that glass," he said. "Please don't break it. Besides, Grayson doesn't need a soaking right now."

Grayson got their point, however. He picked up his wand, pointed it at the far wall, and said, "Clariosity!"

No one said a word, until both Caleb and Sophia burst into laughter.

"Clariosity?" Sophia said. "What was that?"

"I don't know!" Grayson protested. "You guys use words like that, so I just thought that…"

Even Adam was smiling. "The words they use were found in the book," he explained. "I don't think a random word is what works. And not all wands use them anyway. Sometimes, they don't need any at all."

"Oh." Grayson should have remembered that. Bowltre hadn't shouted anything when he was shooting lightning bolts at them. He had in the woods when Grayson first saw him, though, so maybe there was more to it.

"Okay," he finally said. "Maybe I just have to… I don't know… ask it *nicely*?"

"Maybe," Adam said. "Try it."

Grayson nodded and shut his eyes. He didn't want to see his friends' hopeful expressions. Especially not if it didn't work.

He started to talk to his wand silently, in his mind.

"Hi," he said. "I'm don't know if you can hear me. Or what I'm doing. But… are you there?"

Nothing answered him and there was no strong feeling that he was doing the right thing, or the wrong thing, for that matter.

"Okay," he tried again. "I want to know how to make my mom and dad remember me again. Show me how to do that."

But nothing came to him. Grayson kept his eyes closed tight, hoping that something would, but all he felt was his hand starting to ache from being clamped around the wand so tightly.

He opened his eyes. Caleb and Sophia were still staring at him. He met their gazes for a moment, before looking down at his lap. "I'm sorry," he said. "I didn't feel anything."

"That's all right," Caleb grinned. "We're no worse off now than we were before."

"I didn't think it was going to work, anyhow," Sophia said, but she quickly swiped at her eyes with the back of her hand.

"We'll figure it out," Adam said. "I'll keep looking and in the meantime, you keep the wand with you. It's yours now."

"For a few more years, anyway," Caleb added.

"Right." Adam turned back to Grayson. "You can only keep it until you're eighteen years old. After that... well, you see what begins to happen."

Grayson glanced down to Adam's wooden legs, but something felt off about that.

"Wait a minute," he said. "How does Bowltre have a wand then? Or even two of them? Why is he still able to run around?"

Adam sighed and moved to a table to put the book on top of a stack before turning back around.

"The wands did do something to him. Several things, actually. But— unlike me— it wasn't all physical. For Bowltre— Nick, as I used to call him— the damage wasn't to his legs. It was to his mind."

Chapter 17

Adam rolled his chair over to the window and stared out. Grayson looked past him but couldn't see anything out there.

After a while, Adam began to speak.

"Nick and I were two of the first to find the wands. We didn't know where they came from. I stumbled over the first one in the woods. Then, two days later, Nick found another just lying in the dirt outside of his back door. At first, we just laughed about them. They were just kids' toys, after all, and we were getting too old for that sort of thing."

He turned back and regarded them.

"But you all know how it feels. There's something about the wands that makes you want to keep them. Before long, we both had them on us wherever we went. And that made us targets. Bullies don't like anything that's different, and two boys walking around with wooden wands in their pockets were easy prey.

"Or… so they thought. For a little while, we were, and we got the snot kicked out of us a few times. But then, one day, I just sort of took the wand out and said we needed a safe place. I don't know why; it just seemed like the right thing to do. The bullies who were chasing us looked like they ran right into a glass wall. No matter how hard they tried to get to us, they couldn't.

"It was then, of course, that Nick and I realized we had actual, working magic wands. We only needed to find out what Nick's did."

"The lightning?" Grayson asked.

Adam nodded. "The lightning. Once we knew that, Nick wanted to get back at the bullies, but I convinced him that there were better things to do with them. We just didn't know what."

He paused and looked up at the ceiling as a slow smile crept across his face. "Then, Abigail found one. She was one of the prettiest girls in our school. At first, she wanted nothing to do with me and Nick, but then we convinced her that the wands were real. After that, we all became great friends and had a lot of fun together. For the next several years, in fact.

"Once, I found that book—" Adam waved his hand toward the stack where he'd set it. "—on an adventure to a whole different town. This was when we were a little older and there were now five of us. Nick had a car that he was able to use so we could travel farther away.

"When we returned, I started to read it, and realized that there were a lot of these wands, but where they came from and why they suddenly showed up was—and still is—a mystery. But what I did learn for sure was two things: The first was that no one should ever possess more than one wand at a time. If they did, the conflicting nature of them could drive the person crazy.

"The second thing was that the wands had to be given up when the bearer turned eighteen. They had to be given away, or thrown away, or just left somewhere. If not… the book didn't say, but it sure implied that horrible things would happen."

Adam lowered his head, but, to Grayson, it seemed like he wasn't really seeing anything.

"Nick wasn't the oldest of us. He was the second oldest. A guy named Jerry was a couple of months ahead of him, so, as he neared eighteen, he got ready to lose his wand. Nick tried to convince him to give it to him, even though he knew the warning about possessing more than one. Jerry, rightfully so, refused."

"Bowltre took it anyway," Caleb guessed.

"He did." Adam's face hardened. "As soon as Jerry set it down, on his eighteenth birthday, Nick was there. He hit Jerry with a huge lightning bolt. Jerry… well, he was never the same after that. Then

Nick took Jerry's wand and ran off. We didn't see him for a long while."

"Until he came back here after us?" Sophia asked.

"No, earlier than that. He first came back as the rest of us began to turn eighteen. He was already changing. Nick had always been a good-looking kid, but now… his eyes were starting to bulge out of his face and he was fixing his hair in these weird spikes. His voice had gotten rougher, too. He showed up and demanded that all of the wands be turned over to him.

"By then, though, I had figured out how to use my own wand even more effectively than I had before. This house belonged to my parents, so I made it a safe place. Abigail and our other friend left their wands here with me. I've kept them safe ever since. Even though it meant hanging onto my own wand."

"So you have two other wands here?" Caleb sounded like he didn't believe it.

"No," Adam answered. "Over the years, they've disappeared, as mysteriously as they showed up. For a short time, after the last one was gone, I thought maybe I could get rid of mine, finally. But then, Nick reappeared, and I saw him chasing you, Caleb. I knew that it was starting all over again and that my work wasn't done yet."

"What about your parents?" Grayson said. "Did they forget you?"

"No, again, that whole thing is new. I think it's something that Nick is doing. Maybe with another wand he found. At this point, who know how many wands he has."

Grayson thought. Bowltre had gone insane from having too many wands and not giving them up when he should have. He was after theirs and he was doing something— some sort of magic, that must originate from a wand— to make all the adults forget that the kids were even there.

The answer was obvious: get the wands away from Bowltre.

Which meant, they would probably have to kill him.

His stomach twisted into a knot, like it had when he'd told Caleb to close the crack in the street.

Okay. Killing Mr. Bowltre wasn't the answer, then. His stomach relaxed.

But he was still the key to the whole thing. Grayson just had to figure out how.

Chapter 18

"I still don't understand why we don't just stay at Adam's."

It was starting to get dark, and Grayson was walking along the street with Caleb and Sophia. All three had their wands out and at the ready, but Grayson didn't feel any sense of Mr. Bowltre nearby.

"Because we can't do anything there. Besides, Adam gets sort of sensitive about people seeing him trying to do things. He gets weird if we hang out for too long."

"Oh." Grayson could understand that. Even he, at age eleven, didn't want someone watching everything he did.

"We'll go back to the clubhouse," Sophia said. "Hopefully, Sam will have been there and we'll have some food."

"Man, I hope you're right," Caleb said. "I'm starving!"

So far, Grayson had met Caleb and Sophia and had only spoken briefly to Jonah. He'd heard about

Sam, whose wand could apparently bring things to them, while Caleb's wand could break things, and Sophia's could hide them.

"What does Pete do?" he asked.

"Pete? You mean Jonah's wand, Pete?" Caleb laughed. "You're not going to believe it. It makes clouds."

"Clouds?"

"Yep. Clouds."

Grayson couldn't imagine what possible use it could be to own a wand that made clouds. No wonder Jonah had named it Pete. Cloudmaker just didn't sound very cool.

"Is that all of us?" he asked then. "You two, me, Jonah, and Sam?"

"It is now," Sophia answered. "Why?"

"Well, think about it. There's five of us. Adam said that there were five of them. Isn't that kind of funny?"

"I guess so," Caleb shrugged. "But who says we'll stay at five? Maybe someone else is finding a wand right now."

Grayson supposed that was possible, but something about it just felt right. Maybe it was his wand telling him that?

"Do you think there's only five wands then?"

Sophia glanced at him and sneered. "Of course not. We know that already, right? Each of us has one, and that's five. Plus Adam's, then at least two that we know Bowltre has."

"Oh, right." Grayson felt stupid for missing that, but still… there was something about five of them when Adam was young and five of them now…he thought it *must* mean something.

"But what about—?" he started to say, but Sophia cut him off.

"You ask a lot of questions."

Grayson shut his mouth with a snap and the three of them continued to walk along in silence, until Sophia mumbled.

"Sorry. That was rude. My mom always tells me… well, told me… that I could be rude sometimes."

"No problem," Grayson said, but he didn't ask any more questions as they continued.

For the whole trip, Grayson tried to keep alert. He never got any sense from his wand that he was in danger, and he never heard anything that sounded like Mr. Bowltre approaching. Still, he was relieved when the sight of Sophia's house and the relative safety of the clubhouse came into view.

He was even happier when he saw that Jonah was playing in the backyard, along with someone he didn't know.

"Oh, good," Caleb said. "Sam's here. I hope she got some food!"

It took Grayson a moment to realize that Sam was probably short for Samantha. That made three boys and two girls in their club of five. He wondered briefly if Adam's group had been split up the same way. There was only one he hadn't mentioned, so Grayson didn't know if that one was a girl or boy.

Not that it really mattered, he supposed. The whole thing was probably just a weird coincidence anyway.

He suddenly realized that he was lagging behind his other two friends when he heard Sophia say, "Hey, what's that?"

Grayson rushed to catch up and saw what she was asking about.

Jonah and Sam stood on opposite sides of the yard, throwing something, but the other one wasn't trying to catch it. Instead, they were letting it fall to the ground where a low, black shape streaked to retrieve it.

In the gloom of the failing light, it was hard to make out, but Grayson finally saw that it was a longish dog, with wiry black fur, and short legs.

"A dog!" Sophia squealed and ran forward.

"Come on!" Caleb clapped Grayson on the shoulder and ran after her, but Grayson hung back.

He watched and waited, unwilling to go any closer, until he was sure that his stomach wasn't

going to hurt. When he continued to feel perfectly
fine, he crossed the street to the yard as well.

Chapter 19

By the time Grayson caught up, Sophia was already on her knees hugging and playing with the dog, who jumped around her and licked her face.

"He's awesome!" She laughed in delight. "What's his name?"

"I don't know," Sam said. "He was sniffing along the street when I got here."

"I call him Pete," Jonah said proudly.

"He's not Pete!" Sophia huffed. "That's your stupid name for your wand. Why would he be Pete, too?"

Johan shrugged. "I like the name Pete."

"Well, he's not Pete." Sam barely glanced at Jonah as she backed up Sophia. Then, she noticed Grayson. "Oh. You must be the new guy, huh? Jonah told me there was someone else."

"Hey," Grayson nodded to her. "I'm Grayson."

"Not Pete?" she grinned.

Grayson liked her smile. It lit up her face, like whatever she was smiling about was the happiest thought in the whole world. She had long, dark hair that she left loose and was wearing shorts and a t-shirt with a sparkly unicorn on the front. Her skin was darker than Grayson's or Sophia's, but not as dark as Caleb's, and her eyes were a deep brown.

She was the prettiest girl that Grayson had ever seen.

He felt his cheeks burn at that thought and was suddenly glad it was beginning to get dark. To cover his embarrassment, he dropped to his knees next to Sophia and started to pet the dog.

"Grayson just met Adam," Caleb was saying. "And Adam told us more about what happened to him. You wouldn't believe it."

"Sorry I missed that," Sam said. "But I did get some good stuff. Pizza and soda?"

"Yes!" Caleb pounded his fist in the air. "Let's eat!"

Grayson and Sophia rose and they all headed toward the hidden stairs, when Jonah called out, "Wait!"

"What?" Sophia asked when they turned around.

"What about Pete?" Jonah stood by the dog, who looked up at him, then to the others, then back to Jonah.

"He's not Pete," they all said.

Caleb walked back and stood over the dog, looking down at him. The dog sat on it haunches and looked back at Caleb, tongue lolling from its mouth.

"I don't know," Caleb said. "I mean... where did he come from?"

"He's lost," Jonah said. "Look at him. The poor thing hasn't eaten in days."

The dog *was* thin, Grayson had to admit, but it hardly looked like it had been starving.

"Come on, Caleb," Jonah whined. "We can't just leave him out here all night. He'll freeze!"

Jonah was obviously ignoring the fact that it was summertime, and the temperatures at night hardly dipped from the day.

Caleb breathed in deeply and looked back at Sophia. "What do you think?"

"I think he should come in," she said. "At least for now." She scowled at Jonah. "But you're cleaning it up if he makes a mess!"

"No problem," Jonah grinned. "We can just ask Sam to send it away!"

He ran forward, patting his leg and calling, "Come on, Pete!"

The dog trotted after him, answering Jonah's call, whether his name was Pete or not.

Sophia pointed her wand and was opening her mouth, when Grayson stopped her.

"Try it without the word," he said.

She looked at him like he had lost his mind. "Why?"

"Adam said that you don't always need them, remember? Like when Bowltre was firing his lightning at us. I wonder if you could do that, too."

Sophia scowled, but Caleb spoke up. "He's right. Try it. If we can figure out how to do that, we'll have another way to try to fight Bowltre."

"I'll try," she said, "but it's not going to work."

She took a step back and pointed her wand where the cellar stairs were hidden. Nothing happened. She tried again, but still, the stairs didn't appear.

"Told you," she said. This time, she shouted "Reveality!" and the stairs were suddenly there.

Jonah and Sam rushed forward to open them and Sophia followed.

"That was a good idea," Caleb told Grayson.

"Yeah, but it didn't work," he said.

"So what? Not everything does the first time you try it. It's still a good idea to practice. I'm going to try it out later, after I eat a ton of pizza. Want to come with me? Maybe we can figure out something with yours, too."

"Sure!" Grayson said. "That'd be great."

He returned Caleb's grin and followed him down the stairs, where the scent of pizza was already beckoning him.

Chapter 20

For the first time since his mom and dad had forgotten him, Grayson was happy.

Sophia's fears had ended up being for nothing. The dog— and they still couldn't agree on a name other than it *not* being Pete— had jogged down the stairs, sniffed around, and then curled up near the chair and fallen asleep. He hadn't even tried to beg for any pizza.

Grayson sat on one of the couches, slowly eating his fourth slice of pizza and feeling his stomach try to expand to fit it all in. He was overly-full and a little sick feeling, but he didn't think he'd ever been so content. At least for a few minutes.

No one spoke of Adam, or of Mr. Bowltre, or of wands. They talked about superheroes and music and shows on TV, or movies they had seen. No one mentioned the words home, mom, or dad.

Grayson knew it was all temporary, but he was okay with that. For these few minutes, it felt good just to take a break from it all and hang out with his friends.

But eventually, the pizza was gone and so was the soda, and now there wasn't much to do. Outside, it was fully dark, and— if things had been normal— his Mom would have been worrying about where he was. At that thought, the happiness drained out of Grayson, leaving him feeling empty and cold.

The rest of them continued to talk and joke, but Grayson grew quiet. Finally, Caleb turned to him from where he sat on the other end of the couch.

"You don't have to worry," he said. "You can sleep here if you want. Sometimes we do."

Grayson looked around. It wasn't much, really. He could sleep on the floor, he guessed, and maybe Sam could get him a pillow if he asked. But if no one else did, it was going to be creepy.

Not as creepy though, as going home. He didn't know that he could face going into that house and seeing his mom and dad. They'd ignore him or act like they thought they'd heard something but then would shrug and turn away.

He nodded but looked down at his feet.

"Cool," Caleb said. "I'll stay, too."

"Me, too," Sophia said.

"And me," Sam added.

"Me, Pete, and Pete, will be here, too," Johan chimed in.

"His name isn't Pete!" Sophia said, and they all laughed.

Just like that, Grayson felt a little bit better. "Hey," he said to Caleb. "What about practicing?"

"Oh, yeah! I almost forgot." Caleb jumped to his feet. "Let's go back outside. There's more there to break! Anyone else coming?"

No one wanted to, so Grayson was the only one to follow the taller boy outside. Except for the dog, who trailed behind and then sat in the moonlight and watched them.

Caleb looked around and found a few branches that had fallen from nearby trees. He lined them up along the side of the yard and walked back to stand next to Grayson.

"Usually, I point my wand, say the words, and whatever I'm pointing at breaks," he explained.

Grayson thought about it for a moment. "What happens if you miss?"

Caleb stared at him. "I don't," he finally said. "Or at least, I never have."

"Everyone misses sometimes," Grayson answered. "No matter how good you are."

Caleb turned back toward the sticks, but he didn't raise his wand. Instead, he just considered the targets he had lined up.

"You're right," he said. "I guess I never thought about it. I've never missed what I wanted to break, not once. And, as far as I know, Sophia has always hidden whatever she was trying to, and Sam has never pulled the wrong thing to her. Jonah doesn't count. It's hard to screw up a cloud."

Grayson was nodding. "I think the wands somehow know exactly what it is that we're trying to do."

"I'm not sure I like that." Caleb glanced down at his wand. "Does that mean they're alive?"

"I don't think so," Grayson said. "But... maybe. I don't really know."

Caleb raised his wand and pointed it toward the line of sticks. "Here goes," he said.

The snap of a branch breaking in two came clearly from the other side of the yard.

"Wow," Caleb said. "All I did was think it. You were right. You *don't* need the word!"

"So how did you do it?" Grayson asked.

"I just pointed and thought that I wanted to break the second stick from the end. And it did. Just like that."

"Try it without the wand," Grayson said. "Set it down or something."

Caleb frowned but did as Grayson suggested. He looked toward the sticks, but nothing happened, and after a few seconds, Caleb reached down rapidly and grabbed his wand.

"Okay, so we know you have to hold the wand," Grayson said. "Now why don't you try it without pointing."

Caleb tried this one much more readily than he had let go of his wand. But to the same result. None of the sticks broke.

Without waiting for any more suggestions from Grayson, Caleb pointed his wand at the remainder of the sticks in quick succession, jabbing it forward each time like a snake striking at a mouse.

The sticks snapped, one after the other.

"Huh. So you do have to point it," Grayson said. "Interesting."

"Why is that so interesting?" Caleb asked. "It's pretty much what I've been doing all this time."

"Yeah," Grayson agreed. "But mine seemed to work even when it was in my pocket. So… it must be different, right?"

Caleb grimaced. "Right. I think we need to get everyone else up here."

Chapter 21

The other three kids came out when Caleb called down the stairs. He told them what he and Grayson had discovered and asked them all to try their wands the same way he had.

Sophia got the hang of it more quickly, once she saw that Caleb could do it, and realized she had been directing her wand without words anyway. So did Sam, who pulled in a new stack of comic books, one after the other, without uttering a word.

Jonah made a series of clouds, which slowly floated up, until they were lost to view in the darkness.

All of them, though, needed to have their wands out and pointed at what they were trying to affect. Even Jonah and Sam needed to point their wands away from them for the magic to work.

"Maybe it wasn't your wand, after all," Sophia suggested. "Maybe you just guessed right all those times."

"Really?" Caleb scoffed. "So he just guessed right when he told us to run right and then duck just as Bowltre's lightning bolts were coming?"

"Maybe," she shrugged. "What else could it be? He didn't even have his wand out. And besides, he doesn't know how to use it, anyway."

"So maybe his wand *is* different," Sam said.

"Why would that be?" Sophia argued. "We haven't seen any evidence of that."

Caleb and Sam looked like they wanted to continue arguing with Sophia, while Jonah was busy making clouds that hid the dog for a moment before drifting away, but Grayson stopped them.

"It doesn't really matter," he said. "Sophia's right. I don't know how to use it." He took it out and pointed it toward the house. "Show me how to get in," he commanded.

He spoke aloud so the others could hear him.

"Nothing," he said. "There's no feeling that I should go one way or the other. There's no bad feeling that I shouldn't try to climb up on the roof. Nothing."

"We'll get it," Caleb said. "It took us a little while to figure out what Jonah's did too."

Grayson appreciated Caleb's words, but he was pretty sure his wand *was* different. He knew what it did. He'd felt it and, once he'd accepted that, everything had become easier. It was just a matter of making it work all the time now.

He looked down at his wand before sighing and putting it back into his pocket.

"I'm tired," he said. "I think I'm going to get some sleep."

"Good idea," Caleb agreed. "We all should. Let's go."

Deciding to go to sleep on their own felt weird. It wasn't like someone else telling them they had to "go to bed." Or that they had better not stay awake messing around. It was their own decision and it somehow felt like a very grown-up one to make.

He trudged along behind the others as they all went down the stairs. The dog followed him and soon they were all camped out on the couches and floor of the clubhouse. Sam used her wand to get them pillows and blankets for everyone and it was much more comfortable than Grayson had expected. Before he knew it, he fell into a deep sleep.

If he dreamed, he didn't really know it. He did wake up once and sat up quickly, disoriented and scared, until he remembered where he was. The sound of Jonah snoring might have been what had woken him.

Grayson laid back down and stared into the darkness. His eyes slowly adjusted to the light, until he could make out the wood overhead. He wondered what Sophia's mom was doing up there. Was she sleeping peacefully, or did she sense that something was wrong?

That thought made him sad all over again, and he rolled abruptly onto his side.

The dog was awake as well. For a moment, Grayson thought he was staring at him, but then the dog *chuffed* softly before laying his muzzle back onto his paws and closing his eyes.

It took a while, but Grayson finally managed to fall back asleep.

Chapter 22

The next morning, after a breakfast of cold cereal and milk that had Sam pulled in, they tried to decide what they should do with their day.

Jonah voted to just hang-out and play with the dog.

Caleb wanted to practice with his wand. He'd taken Adam's words— that they could get better and better with them— to heart, and he thought everyone else should, too.

Sophia said that they had enough kids now so they could finally play ball. It had been way too long, she said, and Grayson mentioning it the other day had made her miss it.

Sam didn't really care what they did. She was just bored of sitting around.

And Grayson didn't want any of that.

He hadn't slept very well after he finally fell off again. His dreams had been full of his mother and father, and a menacing figure with glowing eyes that stood between them.

While the dreams had been bad, the end result was that he wanted to see his parents again, even if they wouldn't know he was there.

"It's not a good idea," Caleb said. "Trust me."

"I'm going anyway," Grayson told him.

He expected the other boy to argue, but Caleb didn't. Instead, he nodded and said, "All right. I'll go with you. We've all done it, you know? It's just... hard. That's all."

Grayson knew that already. It had been hard the night before last. But he needed to see them, no matter the risk or the result.

They left the others behind and took the walk to Grayson's house. The whole way, they went slowly, waiting for Mr. Bowltre to jump out at them at any moment. But he never did, and Grayson never heard the stomp, drag of his footsteps.

When they arrived, Grayson paused. The house looked different. The boxes that had been stacked in the garage were cleared away, and it was now full of tools and equipment all neatly put in their places. Grayson searched but didn't see any sign of his mitt or bat. There was no bike there, either.

"Where's my stuff?" he asked.

"They probably threw it away without even realizing it," Caleb said. "That's what mine did."

Suddenly, Grayson didn't want to go inside. The thought of seeing his bedroom, even though he'd only slept in it for a couple of nights, empty and all of his stuff gone, was more than he could handle.

"I don't think I want—"

The sound of the front door opening cut him off.

He wasn't going to look. This was a mistake and he was just going to leave.

But, of course, he looked.

His mother and father both came out. His father had his bag that he carried papers back and forth from his office in. His mother was still wearing her housecoat. Both of them looked very happy. They were smiling and laughing, and his mother had ahold of his father's arm. She walked with him to his car and kissed him, then stood and waved cheerfully, while he drove away, tooting the horn twice in goodbye. His mother laughed and walked back into the house.

Not once did either of them notice the two boys, even though they stood right across the street.

The sound of the door closing was a deafening boom to Grayson. The sound of his old life ending forever.

They stood quietly for a minute, until Grayson realized that he was sniffling and his eyes were burning.

"It's okay," Caleb said. He put his long arm around Grayson's shoulder. "Come on. We'll go back to the clubhouse. I think I know what we should do."

They took their time on the way back, allowing Grayson a chance to collect himself and dry his tears. Caleb never said anything about it but chattered on about the neighborhood and the wands and whatever else popped into his head. Twice, he pulled his wand out to crack small rocks on the side of the road into even smaller ones.

Somehow, his ongoing chatter and bright spirit made Grayson feel better. Caleb had been away from his parents longer than Grayson had. He was doing okay. And if he could do it, so could Grayson.

Chapter 23

"We're going back to Adam's," Caleb told everyone a few minutes later.

"Uh-uh." Jonah shook his head. "I told you, I don't like it. He's… weird."

"It's not his fault!" Sophia shot back. "He's only that way because he's keeping a safe place for us!"

"I don't care. He's creepy." Jonah's face was set.

"We're *all* going," Caleb said, as if that settled it.

Which it very well might have. Jonah sat back on the couch with a huff but didn't argue anymore.

"There's something weird going on," Caleb said. "We need Adam's help to figure out what it is."

"What's so weird?" Sam asked.

"Grayson's wand, for one." Caleb motioned to Grayson. "Adam thought he found a picture of it and said that Grayson's wand was a… a wayfinder or something. But, Grayson hasn't been able to make it work."

"Maybe that's just him," Sophia scoffed.

"Maybe it is," Caleb agreed. "But so what? None of us had that much trouble getting them to work.

So why would Grayson? Whether it's the wand or him, it's still a mystery. Plus, there hasn't been any sign of Bowltre since he attacked us yesterday."

"Good!" Jonah crowed. "Maybe he's dead!"

The dog jumped at his sudden outburst, but then settled back down near Jonah's feet.

"He's not," Grayson said. "I don't know how I know. But I do."

"There you go, then," Caleb said. "More mystery. This is big, whatever it is, so I want us all there. Everyone up! We're going."

No one argued anymore, and seconds later, they were back on the street, heading towards Adam's neighborhood.

"Stay sharp!" Sophia said. "Just because we haven't seen Bowltre in a few hours doesn't mean he's not around."

He wasn't. Grayson could have told her that, but he didn't bother. It was enough that they were walking down the sidewalk in safety.

All the way, there was no sign of Bowltre, and the kids moved quickly. Except for Jonah, who lagged behind and had to keep running to catch up when Caleb called him on it. The dog stayed by his side, as if sensing that Jonah needed a little extra comfort.

Grayson dropped back so that he was walking next to the other boy, with the dog between them.

"What do you have against Adam?" he asked.

"Against him? Nothing," Jonah answered. "He just makes me feel weird. With those legs and the stuff all over the house. My dad is really neat, you know? Everything in its place, so it's weird seeing a house like that."

That wasn't the answer, at least the part about the crowded house, that Grayson had expected. Then again, he was just getting to know these kids, so he shouldn't have been surprised.

"I think he's nice," he said. "He tried his best to make me feel comfortable."

"Oh, he's nice. And Sophia is right, he can't help the way he is. But, neither can I."

Grayson couldn't really argue that, although he thought that maybe Jonah *could* try a little harder. Regardless, he was going to have to start soon, because they came around the corner and there was Adam's house.

Sophia had taken the lead and was already at the gate, with Sam right beside her.

Caleb stopped before entering and turned back. "Hurry up!" he called.

Grayson picked up his pace, but Jonah continued to lag behind. Grayson couldn't help smiling when he realized his new friend was stalling like a little kid at bedtime.

"Come on, Jonah!" Sophia yelled.

"I'm coming!" the other boy yelled back.

He's not.

Grayson heard this voice as clear as a bell. More clearly than he'd heard the instruction to veer and duck the day before.

You can't help him. Get inside the fence.

The voice was calm, but Grayson felt a sense of urgency anyway.

"Jonah," Caleb said, "would you hurry up…"

His voice faltered and he stared past Grayson with eyes that were slowly widening.

Grayson didn't stop. He ran forward, grabbed Caleb's arm, and pulled him through the gate. Only then did he let go and spin back.

Jonah was frozen on the street. The dog had latched onto his pant leg and was growling like he'd gotten hold of a burglar.

Then, the dog started to change. He stayed black in color, but his back started to hunch into an arc, and his legs began to lengthen and thicken. The fur on his head began to grow longer and change color, from black to dark green and dim yellow. It formed into spikes as the dog grew bigger, until he started to stand on his back legs, his front legs turning into arms, one of which had a firm hold of Jonah's upper arm.

The dog's growls changed into a harsh, wet laugh, and then, Mr. Bowltre was there.

And he had Jonah.

Chapter 24

The four remaining kids were frozen in place, just as Jonah had been.

It wasn't possible, Grayson thought. If the dog had been Bowltre, why hadn't his wand warned him?

I didn't know, the voice said.

"Let him go!" Caleb yelled. He already had his wand out and pointed at Bowltre.

The hunchbacked man laughed his raspy, wet laugh and lifted his own wand. He'd held it in his left hand, the one not keeping a tight grasp on Jonah's upper arm. Mr. Bowltre raised it and put the tip directly against Jonah's temple.

"Eh?" he said. He tilted his forward-thrusting head to the side. "Do you think you're that fast, boy? Can you break me before I blast this one's head off?"

Caleb wanted to do it. Grayson could see the fury in the other boy's eyes.

"Don't," he said quietly. "Bowltre doesn't want Jonah, or he could have had him already."

"I can break his wand," Caleb whispered.

Do not do that.

The voice spoke inside Grayson's mind again.

"Please, don't," he said aloud to Caleb. "My wand is working again. It's saying not to do that."

"Then what should we do?" Caleb narrowed his eyes, but he lowered his wand slightly and glared at Bowltre. "What do you want?" he yelled.

"Want? Want. Wand…" Mr. Bowltre lingered over the word, almost like he had forgotten what it meant. Even if his mind was distracted though, his hand never wavered, and he kept the lightning wand pointed at Jonah's temple.

Finally, he seemed to come back to himself. "For starters… this!"

He reached down quickly with the hand still holding his wand and pulled Jonah's from his grasp.

Several things happened at once.

Jonah cried out, sounding for all the world like he had lost his best friend. "Pete! No!"

Mr. Bowltre now had two wands visible, both held in one hand. He threw his head back and howled.

That howl was one of the loudest, most confusing sounds Grayson had ever heard. He clapped his hands over his ears but the noise came through anyway. It was a howl of triumph, of victory, but tarnished by great pain.

Mr. Bowltre howled again and let go of Jonah to transfer one of the wands to that hand.

When he did, Sam jumped forward, as close to the low stone wall as she could and jabbed her wand out.

"Summoniosity!" she yelled.

Jonah flew through the air, directly toward Sam, like he was attached to a string. When he got to the wall, his feet clipped the top, and he tumbled into her, sending them both crashing to the ground.

Out on the street, Bowltre had put one of the wands away. It was Pete, Grayson saw, since Bowltre still held the lightning wand.

Worse than that, though, Bowltre was staring directly at him. His protruding eyes seemed to have grown even bigger. He glared at Grayson and shivered, then ran a dark tongue over his lips.

"Give it, boy," he snarled. His voice had become even deeper and wetter. "Give it, and I'll return the other brat's to him."

Grayson looked down at his wand, then over at Jonah. He didn't appear to be hurt by his impact with the wall, but was curled up on the ground, sobbing harshly. Sam was trying to console him.

Do not do it. He lies.

Grayson didn't need the voice to tell him that. If he gave up his wand, then Bowltre wouldn't stop until he had Caleb's, and then Sophia's, and then

Sam's. He wasn't going to ever be content until he had them all.

"How did you do it?" Grayson surprised himself by yelling to Bowltre. "How did you stay hidden?"

Mr. Bowltre laughed. "So smart. So stupid. So young. So old."

"What's that supposed to mean?" Sophia shouted.

"Nothing," a voice said from behind them.

Grayson spun around. Adam was on the porch, and he held a wand of his own.

It was made of wood polished so brightly it shone like gold. Adam had it held pointed straight up, and his face was set in a determined expression.

"It means nothing," he repeated. "Nick is insane. He's not in touch with reality anymore. Come inside, all of you. I don't think he can push his way in here, but…"

But somehow he'd already hidden from Grayson's wand, so who knew what he was capable of now?

Bowltre began to laugh again and this time it grew louder and higher pitched. "Adam!" He sounded as if he were greeting a long-lost friend. "Adam! I've missed you! Where are they, Adam? Where are the others? I see yours. It looks like it's wonderful. Let me see it…"

His voice trailed off into muttering and snarls, and he moved closer.

Stomp, drag.

Bowltre ignored the kids and smiled at Adam. Drool ran over his chin.

Stomp, drag.

He was at the gate.

Grayson and the others backed up slowly, moving toward the porch and Adam. Sam dragged a still-sobbing Jonah to his feet and pulled him along.

Stomp, drag.

Mr. Bowltre grabbed a hold of the gate.

Chapter 25

When Mr. Bowltre's hand made contact with the low, iron gate, there was a hot, sizzling sound, like bacon frying in a pan. He grimaced but didn't let go.

On the porch, Adam grabbed his wand with two hands and frowned. His eyebrows drew down as he concentrated on keeping Mr. Bowltre from being able to open the gate.

Go help him.

Grayson didn't question what the wand was telling him to do. He ran up the stairs to the porch and behind Adam. He put his hand on Adam's shoulder and looked back at the gate and Mr. Bowltre, who was still snarling and pushing on it.

Something went through Grayson. He wasn't sure what it was, but he felt different, like everything that was happening was far away. He thought he heard a voice. Maybe it was his wand, but it was very faint. It was a whisper he could barely hear and then... something else seemed to answer it.

The spitting, frying sound grew louder, until there was a sudden crack, a lot like the noise the lightning made when Bowltre cast it from his wand. A brilliant white flash brought Grayson's attention back to what was going on around him.

He blinked his eyes rapidly, trying to clear the after-effects of the flash.

Mr. Bowltre was lying on the street in a heap, the leg he dragged stiffly sticking out. Smoke rose from his coat.

"Is he dead?" Sophia whispered.

No one moved or said a word. Their eyes stayed glued to the unmoving figure crumpled on the ground.

With a sudden, loud gasp of breath, Mr. Bowltre rose to his feet, almost as if he had been pulled upright by some invisible hand. He snarled and spun back to them.

His mouth worked and his hands twitched. He bent down to pick up the lightning wand, which had landed beneath him when he was thrown back.

Adam didn't say a word.

They stared at each other, until Mr. Bowltre began to move away. He shuffled backward at first, keeping his large eyes fixed on Adam the whole way, until he twisted around and lurched off.

Stomp, drag. Stomp, drag.

The noise of his retreat receded, until finally, it had disappeared entirely.

"Is he really gone?" Sam asked.

Grayson waited, but his wand remained silent.

"He's gone," Adam answered. "Although… he almost had me." He twisted around so that he could see Grayson behind him. "You did something. What was it?"

Grayson only shrugged. "I don't know. My wand told me to help you… so I did."

"More feelings?" Adam asked.

"No," Grayson replied. "Not anymore. Now it *is* words."

Adam stared at him for a second, his face motionless. Then he turned away and put his hands on the wheels of his chair. "Come. Everyone. Inside, now."

He pushed himself around Grayson and to the still-open front door.

Sophia dashed in after him. Sam had her arm around the still weeping Jonah and led him in as well.

"Your wand is speaking to you?" Caleb hadn't moved from the foot of the stairs. He was staring up at Grayson like he didn't want to come near him.

Grayson nodded. "Yeah. It just started when we were close to here. Right before Bowltre changed."

"Weird timing," Caleb said.

"Yeah." Grayson didn't know what his friend was getting at.

Neither of them moved.

"Are you going inside?" Grayson finally asked.

Caleb nodded this time. "After you."

Grayson didn't like the way Caleb was looking at him. It was like the other boy thought he had done something wrong, or wasn't being honest, or... well, Grayson didn't know. But something.

He didn't say any of that, though. Instead, he just turned away and followed the others inside the house.

Chapter 26

By the time he entered, the other kids and Adam were already gathered in the round tower room.

Adam was seated behind a desk with "Lost Wands" open in front of him. He was paging through it slowly, his lips working soundlessly the whole time.

Jonah sat on a small sofa, which had been hastily cleared off, with Sophia and Sam on either side of him. He wasn't crying any more, but his face was red and he was sniffling. A large, dark bruise was already forming on his upper arm where Mr. Bowltre had grabbed him.

When Grayson entered, Adam glanced up and noticed him, then slowly sat back in his chair.

"What did you mean?" He asked after a few uncomfortable moments had dragged by.

"About what?" Grayson knew what the man meant, but he suddenly felt uncomfortable talking about it.

"About your wand. You say it actually spoke to you? With words, not just feelings?"

Grayson swallowed hard and nodded.

"I see," Adam said. "And when did this first start?"

"Right before Bowltre grabbed Jonah," Caleb said from behind Grayson. "At least, that's what he told me."

Grayson still didn't understand why Caleb was so upset, but he was already starting to get tired of it.

"What's your problem?" He rounded on Caleb.

"Problem? Nothing? Why do you think there's a problem?"

"Because there is," Grayson spat. "So just say it."

Caleb glared at him, but then stepped around him to find a chair that he could clean off to sit in. "No problem," he said casually. "I just think it's *funny* that this suddenly happened. When we all know that you couldn't make your wand work before. Now it works when you're not even holding it? Which none of us can do? It's just odd, that's all."

"You think I'm faking it?" Grayson couldn't believe his ears.

Caleb shrugged. "Maybe you didn't want to be the one left out anymore."

"I don't want to be here at all!" Grayson shouted. "I want to be home. With my Mom and

Dad! And not in this stupid place, but back where we used to live. Back where my friends are!"

His eyes burned and he was shouting, but, in a way, it felt good, too.

All the frustration at having to move, all the anger at living in such a weird place, and all the fear that he'd never have his mother and father again seemed to flow out of him.

Caleb sat stunned by his outburst. The other three kids were staring at him, as well.

But Adam sat quietly, giving Grayson a chance to calm down.

"He's not faking it, Caleb," Adam finally said. "I don't know about the voice, but Grayson isn't a liar. I do know that he somehow helped me out there. If it wasn't for what he did— whatever it was— Nick would have gotten in."

"But how is that?" Sophia asked. "Your wand makes a safe-space, right? No one can get in who you don't want to."

"Exactly," Adam confirmed. "But, somehow, Nick felt stronger. He's never done that before. I suspect…" He trailed off for a moment. "Well. I think maybe he found another wand. One that's making him stronger than he ever was."

"What about changing into the dog?" Jonah's voice was low and full of bitterness. "How did he do that?"

Adam shook his head. "I don't know. Nick has been searching for and collecting wands for a long time now. But that doesn't mean he always knows what they do. Maybe he's had one that lets him change shape for a while, but only recently figured it out. That's just a guess though."

It's more than that.

Grayson cleared his throat. "Um. I think it might be more than that. There's something else."

"How do you know that?" Caleb asked. "Your wand speak to you?"

His voice was mocking, but Grayson chose to ignore that. "Yes," he answered simply. "Just now."

Caleb scowled and looked away.

Adam took a deep breath. "Then I'll continue looking." He put his hand on the book in front of him. "This book is... hard to read. It's not organized in any certain way that I can tell. A lot of the words are so old I'm not always sure what they mean. Some of the pages are dirty or torn. But I'm convinced the answers are in here." He frowned. "I just wish people had taken better care of it over the years."

It has always looked like that, the voice said.

Grayson kept that to himself.

Chapter 27

It was good to sit in a place where they were all safe. Mr. Bowltre had gone away, at least for the moment, and Grayson hoped he wouldn't be back to test Adam's magic again.

He won't be, his wand told him. *That was quite a shock he got.*

Grayson stayed quiet. In fact, his wand had made a few comments since they'd gained the safety of Adam's house. For something that he couldn't get to work at all earlier, it seemed like his wand didn't want to shut-up now.

But Grayson didn't want to say anything more about it. Caleb was still being weird, even though Grayson didn't understand why. Caleb talked with the other kids while Adam kept paging through "Lost Wands," but anytime Grayson tried to add anything, he either scoffed at it or simply didn't answer.

Finally, Grayson had had enough. He stood up and walked over to where Caleb was talking with Sophia.

"Can I talk to you?" he said.

Caleb looked up at him, his eyebrows drawn down angrily. For a second, Grayson thought he was going to say no or that he was going to say something mean, but before he could, Sophia shoved Caleb just enough to rock him to the side.

"Stop being a jerk," she said. "Whatever your problem is, it's not Grayson's fault."

Caleb swiveled to face her, a retort rising to his lips, but he stopped at the calm, determined expression Sophia met him with.

"Fine," he mumbled. He climbed to his feet and stood looking down at Grayson, but he didn't move.

Grayson sighed. Caleb wasn't going to make this easy.

He walked out of the room and toward the kitchen of Adam's house, aware of Caleb following closely behind. When they were away from the others, it suddenly occurred to Grayson that Caleb was older and much bigger than he was. He swallowed hard and resisted the urge to look back until they had entered the kitchen.

Caleb now sounded more bored than aggressive as he said, "So? What do you want?"

"What did I do wrong?" Grayson asked him. He had meant to keep his voice level, to show Caleb that he was tough, too, and that even though he didn't like whatever was happening between them, it didn't *really* bother him. Only, his words came out much more plaintively than he had intended. He heard himself and he sounded like a big baby.

Caleb seemed to think so, too. *"What did I do wrong?"* he repeated, and he turned Grayson's words into even more of a whine. Then he laughed. "You know what you did."

Grayson didn't. He wracked his brain as he thought back, trying to remember what he could have done to make Caleb so mad at him.

"Is this all because my wand is speaking to me?" he finally asked.

He couldn't really believe that was the problem. Why would it be? With everything else that had been happening, with all the amazing things they could do, why would that make Caleb mad?

"Just stop the act," Caleb spat. "Whatever is going on with your wand, great. It's helping you to avoid danger. Helping us all, I guess, that's cool. That's awesome. But you never said anything about it talking to you until Adam put the idea in your head last time we were here. Now suddenly your wand does? It just doesn't make sense."

"But why would I make that up?" Grayson asked him.

"Because you were tired of being the only one who couldn't make your wand work. You were... I don't know... jealous or something."

That took Grayson by surprise so much that he started to laugh.

"What's so funny?" Caleb demanded.

"The thought that I'm jealous. I don't even know what's going on, really. I'm *not* jealous." He hesitated. "I'm scared. All right?"

His cheeks started to burn and he had to turn away from Caleb. He didn't want to see the disgust he knew the other boy would look at him with.

But Caleb didn't say anything for a minute and then, in a quiet voice, said, "Well. I'm scared too, you know. So are Sophia and Sam. Even Jonah is scared, but he covers it by being silly."

"Then why are you so mad at me?" Grayson turned back. "I'm not making up hearing my wand. I wish I didn't even have one!"

Caleb seemed to shrink in on himself and leaned against the counter. He crossed his arms and wouldn't look at Grayson.

"Honestly. . . because if your wand is going to be telling us what to do, no one will need me anymore."

Grayson couldn't believe it. Caleb was the most confident, natural leader Grayson had ever met. When he'd told them all that they were going to

Adam's, even Jonah hadn't said no. And Caleb was the one who stood up to Mr. Bowltre, who would have fought him when he held Jonah.

To disastrous effect, his wand said.

Grayson ignored the voice. He wasn't even sure what it meant.

"You're the leader," he finally said. "You know that. My wand will just be… I don't know… back up? Another way for us to know how to beat Bowltre?"

Caleb glanced at Grayson, then dropped his eyes. Finally, he nodded. "Yeah. I'm… sorry."

"It's okay," Grayson shrugged, suddenly uncomfortable. "Sometimes, we just get…"

He ran out of words, but it didn't really matter. He'd smoothed things over with Caleb. They could still be friends. And now that was out of the way, and they could concentrate on Mr. Bowltre.

Chapter 28

Grayson had expected Sophia to make a comment when he and Caleb returned to the round room, but she was busy looking at a book with Jonah.

Ever since losing his wand, Jonah had alternated between being angry, being too quiet, or simply crying. At the moment, he sat and stared dully at the pages as Sophia turned them, looking for all the world like a small child being read a story when they were too sleepy to really pay attention to it.

Sam had dozed off on the other end of the couch, and Adam was still looking through his own book.

"I think we should concentrate first on getting Pete back," Grayson announced to the room in general.

They all looked at him like he had made some sort of horrible joke. Even Adam paused in his reading and Sam stirred.

"What...? Why...?" Sophia didn't seem to know what to say.

"That's right," Caleb said. He stepped up next to Grayson. "That's what we were talking about."

"But… what about getting your parents to remember you?" Adam said. "I thought that was most important?"

"It was," Grayson said. "And it's still important. But… well, Mr. Bowltre didn't have any right to take Jonah's wand. That's stealing, like he accuses us of doing."

Adam nodded slowly. "I understand." He sighed. "I suppose it's not a bad idea. Not in the long run. Nick must have at least a few wands now, to do the things he's been doing. I still don't know how he's making your parents forget you. I suspect it's magic like my safe space, or Sophia's ability to hide things like your clubhouse. Spells that will work over time, rather than all at once, like Caleb's breaking things."

Huh. That was yet another aspect of the wands that Grayson hadn't thought of. Some magic seemed to last for a long time, maybe forever. But others were instant. There and then gone. Once Caleb broke something, it broke and that was it. It didn't keep breaking. The same with Sam's wand. It didn't keep on bringing her the item she asked for. If she wanted more, she had to use it again.

"That's how he changed into a dog," Grayson said. "But... it still doesn't explain how he hid from my wand."

He waited, but his wand stayed silent.

"Anyway," he continued. "We have to get Pete back. That's first. Then we can concentrate on anything else."

"Good plan," Adam agreed. "I'll keep working with the book. Let me know what you all come up with."

He smiled at them, stuck a piece of paper in the book to mark his place, and then leaned back, stretched his arms overhead, and opened his mouth in a tremendous yawn.

"All right, time to go," Caleb said.

This time, everyone except for Adam, looked at Caleb like he was crazy.

"Go where?" Sam asked.

"I don't know," Caleb said. "Back to the clubhouse, I guess."

"We can't," Jonah said. "Bowltre knows where it is!"

"Oh, right." Caleb frowned. "Well... maybe we can go to one of our houses. We could just sort of hang out in one of our old bedrooms or something, right? It's not like they would notice."

"Whose house?" Grayson asked.

He didn't want it to be his. He didn't want his mom and dad looking right through him. He didn't think he could take that.

And neither, apparently, did anyone else.

"Adam, do you have any ideas?" Grayson asked.

Adam only shook his head and yawned again, which made Grayson annoyed.

"What a minute," he said. "It doesn't matter if Bowltre knows where the clubhouse is. He still can't get in. Without Sophia showing him, he can't find the doors. Remember? I was sitting right on top of them and didn't even know it."

"True," Caleb said. "But he'll be watching for us to leave here. And he'll know where we're going."

Caleb was right. Mr. Bowltre *would* be watching. He did know where they were now and where they would probably go.

What he didn't know, though, was when.

"I think I have an idea," Grayson said.

Chapter 29

Like most houses, Adam's had a back door. His opened to a backyard that was overgrown with shrubs and plants that had gotten out of control. The door hadn't been opened in years. The deadbolt lock was hard to turn, and the door itself was so stuck in its frame that Caleb and Sophia had to yank on it together before it finally popped open.

Beyond the yard was a narrow lane, with another backyard, which was much more neatly maintained, across from Adam's. A man was mowing the lawn in the bright afternoon light, but he never looked over at the door opening or at the small group of kids now standing in the backyard.

"All right," Caleb said. "What's the idea?"

They spoke in hushed tones, in case Mr. Bowltre was anywhere around.

"Bowltre is probably watching the front of the house," Grayson answered. "He can't be in both places at once and since you guys have always gone that way, that's where he'll be."

"Makes sense," Sam said. "So now what? We just try to sneak down the road before he sees us?"

"No. I think he's tracking us somehow. Smell, maybe?" Grayson turned to Sophia. "You told me that your wand can hide something completely, but I'm guessing you never thought about smell. Do you think it could do that, too? If you told it that's what you wanted?"

She shrugged. "I don't know, really. I mean, I guess so?"

"That's going to have to be good enough," Grayson said. He took a deep breath. "We're all going to walk together, and Sophia is going to hide us as we go."

"What? I can't do that!" she cried.

"Why not?" Grayson asked her.

"Because I can only hide things that are still! And I don't know that I can hide all of us at one time anyway. There's too many!"

"You can," Caleb said. "I get what Grayson is talking about. You can do it, Sophia. You're stronger than you think."

"Besides," Grayson added. He glanced at Caleb, hoping that what he was about to say wasn't going to make him angry. "I'm going to help you."

Caleb nodded. "Like he did with Adam."

Grayson breathed a sigh of relief that Caleb had joined in with him.

"You heard him," Caleb continued. "Whatever Grayson did helped make Adam strong enough to hold Bowltre off. He can do the same for you."

He looked at Grayson and nodded once. Grayson smiled in return.

"Yeah. Just like that. It'll be easy."

"Right?" He asked silently.

I can help, his wand answered.

"I don't know," Sophia said. "I'm not sure I can…" She stopped and looked at them all, and then determination crept over her face. "No. I can do this."

She took her wand out of her shirt and held it point up, the same way that Adam had.

"Imagine we're under a big, upside-down glass bowl," Caleb said helpfully.

"No, like a bubble," Jonah said. "Maybe we'll move faster if we're rolling."

"Maybe one of you would like to do this?" Sophia snapped.

Everyone fell silent and Sophia closed her eyes. After a moment, she opened them. "Okay. I think we're good."

They gathered in a circle around her and walked out of the backyard and into the alley. Grayson took his wand out and slowly waved it back and forth in front of him.

What are you doing?

"Making sure Bowltre isn't around," Grayson replied silently.

You don't need to do that.

"I want to."

Suit yourself. If it was possible for a wand to sound annoyed, this one was.

Still, it made Grayson feel better to do it, so he kept at it.

They cautiously made their way out of the lane and back to the street they knew, coming onto it several houses down from Adam's. They stopped and looked both ways, searching for any sign of Bowltre, but they didn't see anything. Grayson's wand never spoke to him, either.

When they had a gone a little farther, Grayson noticed that Sophia's hands, both of which were clasped tightly around her wand, were beginning to tremble. Her arms were drooping a little.

Like he had with Adam, Grayson stepped closer and put his hand on her shoulder. He got that same disconnected feeling, like he was watching his own body move down the street with his friends. It only lasted for a few seconds though, and then Sophia seemed to get a boost of strength. Her arms came up and her trembling stopped.

"Thanks," she said and glanced at him with a quick smile.

"No problem," he replied.

Even inside of Sophia's magic, they spoke quietly.

Then, the sound they'd all been dreading reached them.

Stomp, drag. Stomp, drag.

Mr. Bowltre appeared from next to a house, clomping down the driveway directly toward them. He was muttering and growling, and his eyes were roving back and forth, but he didn't seem to see them.

Every few steps, he stopped and sniffed loudly, but even that didn't lead him to the group.

They stopped moving, all of them staring at Mr. Bowltre, willing him not to see, or smell, them.

"Here. They're not there. So they're here. Somewhere. Between there and there. Not here. There."

Bowltre kept up a running commentary of nonsense, swinging between almost normal speech and a guttural, dog-like growl. He passed within two feet of Caleb, but never noticed him standing there.

Grayson almost smiled. It was like his mom and dad again, only this time, he had never been so glad to be ignored.

They watched as Mr. Bowltre dragged his leg up the street.

But their grins faded when they realized he was heading the same way they were. Directly back toward the clubhouse.

Chapter 30

The group stayed far back from Mr. Bowltre as he made his lurching way to Sophia's house. Once there, he looked around and sniffed once more, moved from the sidewalk to stand next to a house, and then pulled a wand from his coat. He pointed it, only this time, he pointed at himself, and then, in the blink of an eye, he disappeared.

Everyone froze, unsure of what to do.

"Now what?" Sam hissed. "We don't know where he is!"

"No," Grayson said. "This isn't like Sophia hiding something. He's just invisible. We can still hear him if he comes for us."

"Maybe," Caleb said. "But he doesn't need to be near us to hit us with his lightning wand."

"Guys?" Sophia's voice was shaky. "I don't mean to be a baby, but I'm getting really tired."

Her arms were trembling again, even though Grayson hadn't let go of her shoulder. As a matter of fact, now that she mentioned it, Grayson was starting to feel like he could lie down and take a quick nap himself.

"What's going on?" he silently asked.

His wand didn't answer, and now that he thought about it, it hadn't given him any indication that Mr. Bowltre was nearby, either. Maybe it could only do one thing at a time?

"We have to hurry," he said. "Let's keep moving."

"There's a problem," Sophia said. "I can't keep us all hidden and un-hide the doors at the same time."

"Oh." Grayson hadn't thought of that.

"We need Bowltre to go away," Caleb said. "Let me try something."

He pulled his wand from his pocket and pointed it at a window in the house that they hoped Mr. Bowltre still stood near. The window shattered suddenly, and a scream came from inside the house.

Grayson felt a little bad about breaking someone's window, but if it drove Mr. Bowltre off, it was worth it.

They didn't hear Mr. Bowltre's footsteps, however. In fact, there was nothing at all, except the woman who lived in the house looking out in bewilderment.

"It didn't work," Sam said.

"We really have to hurry," Sophia said. Her breath was starting to come in quick pants and her wand was beginning to dip.

"Keep moving," Caleb said. "I'll distract him."

"How are you going to—" Jonah asked, but before he could finish, Caleb took off running.

There was a sudden howl from thin air. The woman in the window jumped back with a scream and then Mr. Bowltre was there. He raised the lightning wand and pointed it at the fleeing Caleb.

The rest of them hurried across Sophia's yard.

The lightning bolt flashed out of Mr. Bowltre's wand, but Caleb had taken him by surprise and had already turned a corner. The lightning hit a house instead with a tremendous crack that made the woman scream again.

"Shut up," Bowltre growled and looked up at her.

The kids stopped near the hidden doors.

"Now what?" Grayson asked impatiently.

But Sam had turned and was watching Mr. Bowltre carefully. She saw what he was about to do next. Grayson followed her gaze, just in time to see Bowltre snarl and point his wand at the woman in the window.

"No!" Sam jabbed her wand at Bowltre's.

It wasn't much. There must have been too much attachment for her to pull the lightning wand from his hand, but it was enough to throw off his aim. Instead of hitting the woman, the lightning bolt flashed by the side of the house. Grayson didn't see what it actually hit.

The woman kept screaming, even louder now, and Mr. Bowltre cursed and hurried away, muttering to himself.

Sophia began to sway and Grayson held onto her, but he was getting more and more tired himself.

"Can't do it anymore," she mumbled.

"Just a little bit," Grayson encouraged.

Mr. Bowltre was rushing down the street, in the same direction Caleb had gone, as fast as his bad leg would allow. The woman who had nearly been hit was gone from the window. Grayson imagined she was inside, calling the police.

It was enough. He dropped his hand from Sophia's shoulder.

"The doors," he said weakly.

She nodded, let her wand drop, and pointed it before falling over.

The doors were there, and Sam and Jonah hurried to open them. They each took one of Sophia's arms and helped her up, then half carried her as they staggered down the stairs.

Grayson stayed where he was, holding his wand and blinking furiously.

"What are you doing?" Jonah asked him. "Get in here!"

"Not yet," Grayson said. "Caleb isn't back."

"He can take care of himself!"

"No." Grayson shook his head. "I have to help him."

He shook off his weariness and walked purposefully across the yard, turning after Mr. Bowltre as soon as he was on the street.

Somewhere off in the distance, but getting closer, was the sound of police sirens.

Chapter 31

At first, Grayson tried to stay hidden as he ran, sure that the police would want to know what he was doing and what he knew about the broken window. Then he remembered that police were adults, too, and they weren't going to notice him anymore than his parents did. After that, he ran as fast as his tired legs would go.

He wasn't sure where Caleb had run off to. If he was going to try to distract Mr. Bowltre, then it would make sense that he stayed in sight, at least for a second or two at a time, so that he could lead Bowltre away, while still not getting hit by the lightning.

Slow down.

Grayson slowed to a walk, keeping his eyes and ears open.

"Is he near?" he asked the wand.

Yes. Around the next corner. He's invisible again.

"What do I do, then?" Grayson asked.

Keep going. He can only use one wand at a time.

Grayson walked slowly now and turned the corner so that he could see all the way down the next street. Neat houses lined the road, with cars parked in most of the driveways. Nobody was around, though. Not anyone from any of the houses, not Mr. Bowltre, and not Caleb.

"Maybe I should go back to the clubhouse," Grayson whispered.

No. Stay for a moment. I'm trying to...

The wand fell silent. Grayson slowed his pace even more, until he was barely moving. He strained hard to hear Mr. Bowltre's footsteps.

Then, he saw a flicker of movement. It was there, and then gone again, so quickly that Grayson wasn't sure he'd seen it. Then it came again. On the opposite side of the street, several houses up from where Grayson stood. A dark shape, but brighter at the top, flickered into sight, then was gone. It happened yet again, and Mr. Bowltre stayed visible longer this time.

He was glaring at Grayson and moving almost as slowly. He put his good leg down carefully, then slowly drew his other forward, so that it hardly made any sound at all.

Ah. There it is. Now, give me a moment more.

Grayson wasn't sure that he had a moment. Mr. Bowltre was moving toward him, his mouth working like he was speaking, but if he was, he was doing it so quietly that Grayson couldn't hear him. Then, he stopped and pushed his head even farther forward. If it was possible for his large, bugged-out eyes to narrow, they did.

"You see me, boy." His growl wasn't a question.

And Grayson did see him now. Fully. No more flickering. Mr. Bowltre in all his glory, with his spiked green and yellow hair, his dirty black coat, and his heavy boots. He held a wand in a reverse grip, so that it was pointed at him.

When Grayson didn't respond, but also didn't turn away like he *didn't* see Mr. Bowltre, the man growled again. He moved the wand so that it was no longer pointed at him, and, instantly, it was even easier to see him. His arm moved smoothly to tuck the wand inside his coat, and when his hand came out, he held another.

Time to go, Grayson's wand said. *No need to run. But walk quickly.*

Everything inside Grayson was telling him that he *did* need to run! He recognized the wand Mr. Bowltre now held. Long, slim, black, with a gold line along it, it was the lightning wand. If he didn't dodge, Mr. Bowltre was going to fry him where he stood!

No, he won't. Don't run, don't try to dodge. Simply walk.

"But—" Grayson began to protest.

Just do as I tell you, the wand replied. *I'll explain later.*

Grayson nodded and did what the wand told him. He couldn't help flinching when a lightning bolt streaked by to sizzle into the lawn on his right. Another crashed to the left of him.

"I'll have you yet, boy!" Mr. Bowltre's snarl came clearly from behind Grayson.

Another lightning bolt, this time closer, but not so near that it affected him.

Okay, you can run whenever you wish, the wand said.

Grayson ran. He lowered his head, pumped his arms, and ran as fast as he ever had.

Bowltre let loose with one of his disturbing howls. Grayson glanced back, just in time to see Mr. Bowltre tuck the lightning wand away and take out another.

"Please be Pete," Grayson muttered.

It wasn't Pete. It was one Grayson hadn't seen before. This one was a bit shorter and fatter than the others, made of a dark wood. Mr. Bowltre pointed it at himself, muttering the whole time, and passed the wand down his body, starting at his head.

He started to change, again. He dropped to all fours and his coat seemed to be absorbed into his skin, while dark hair began to sprout all along his body, except for along his back, where the black hair stood up in green and yellow spikes. His nose and mouth pushed forward, turning his flat, human face into one with a muzzle.

Grayson kept staring, which made him stumble as he continued to run.

Stop looking, the wand told him. *Just run now.*

But Grayson couldn't help it. Mr. Bowltre had become a dog again. But it wasn't the same dog. This one was much bigger, with long legs and a powerful chest. This was a dog built for running down prey.

And you're the prey, his wand warned him. *Now move.*

Chapter 32

Grayson had never run so fast in his entire life.

The Bowltre-dog let out a furious growl, sounding more like an animal than any other time Grayson had heard it.

Then, there was silence. Grayson would have expected the dog to be barking as it chased him, but he didn't hear anything at all.

He glanced back, sure that maybe the dog had run off another way or wasn't even chasing him after all.

He was. And he was running much faster than Grayson could have even if he hadn't been so tired.

Grayson couldn't take his eyes off of the dog. It was almost hypnotic to watch its movements, and besides, if he turned around, he'd have no warning when it was on him. The first he would know of it catching him would be when its big teeth sank into his leg or his arm!

Stop. He's not going to catch you. Just keep running.

Grayson trusted the wand, so turned forward, and tried to move faster.

But he was so tired! For a few moments, the excitement of finding Mr. Bowltre and seeing that he hadn't caught Caleb had almost made him forget his exhaustion, but now it took so much effort to *just keep moving*. He was slowing down and no matter how hard he tried, he couldn't force himself to go any faster.

Now he could hear the dog. Sharp nails scratched on the hard concrete of the sidewalk as it neared. Grayson knew that if he could hear that, dog-Bowltre was right behind him. He sobbed and tried to run faster.

Sharp teeth closed on his leg. It was only a nip; dog-Bowltre wasn't quite close enough to get a full bite, but it was enough.

With a startled shriek, Grayson stumbled forward, falling to his knees and skinning them badly. Before he could even think of getting up, dog-Bowltre plowed into him, knocking him flat and slamming his chin to the concrete.

Stars flashed in Grayson's vision and he thought he was going to be sick.

But dog-Bowltre was still there. He'd flown over Grayson when he'd knocked him down but was scrabbling for purchase on the hard sidewalk as he turned around. His muzzle was stretched back to reveal huge teeth and drool ran from his jaws, just as it did with human-Bowltre.

Grayson screamed again and threw himself back, just as dog-Bowltre lunged toward him.

Roll back. Like a backward somersault. Keep going.

In his panic, Grayson almost didn't hear the wand, but he tried to do it anyway.

He made a clumsy back-somersault, not worrying about what was behind him. He veered off to one side as he continued rolling and found that the curb was closer than he'd realized. His breath exploded out of him as he rolled off the sidewalk and onto the street.

There was a tremendous crack, so loud it hurt Grayson's ears, and a sudden yelp from dog-Bowltre.

Grayson shook his head and tried to get up, but he was dizzy from the rolling, the smack of his chin on the concrete, and the terror of the dog-Bowltre attack.

He staggered to his feet and gaped at what he saw in front of him.

The entire sidewalk was gone! It had collapsed into a huge hole. For many feet to both Grayson's left and right, the only thing remaining was a gaping chasm in the earth.

He cautiously shuffled forward and peered over the edge. It was deep. So deep that it was almost dark at the bottom, but, as his eyes adjusted to the gloom, he thought he could see something moving.

After a moment, Mr. Bowltre's voice floated up to him.

"Get you yet, boy. My wand. You all have my wands. Take them all."

He was muttering and spitting at the bottom of a long, narrow pit. Mr. Bowltre must have taken quite the fall when the chasm opened, and yet, he was still alive, still threatening them.

He was just starting away when he heard, "Is he dead?"

Grayson wasn't surprised when Caleb stepped up next to him.

"No," he said. "He's down there, alive and angry."

"I didn't think so," Caleb sighed. "Are you all right?"

The back of Grayson's leg stung where dog-Bowltre had nipped him, his knees burned from where he'd fallen, and, worst of all, his chin felt like he had been hit with a hammer. And his head was pounding.

"I'm okay," he lied.

Caleb looked back at the huge crack he'd made and whistled. "Wow. I never did anything that big before. I wasn't sure it would work."

Grayson could only nod, grateful that it had.

"Let's get back to the clubhouse," Caleb whispered, so Mr. Bowltre couldn't hear him.

"Sophia can hide it again and we'll be safe for the night."

Grayson nodded. Sleep would be great, he thought. He was more tired than he could ever recall being.

He didn't want to think about the morning, though. Mr. Bowltre would know where they were hiding. He might not be able to get in, but that didn't mean he wouldn't be there waiting when they came out. And, unlike Adam's house, there was no back door to sneak out of.

Chapter 33

It was quiet in the clubhouse. Everyone was either lost in their own thoughts or too tired to talk.

Grayson was both. There was something bothering him that he was hesitant to bring up to the rest of them. Well, there was a lot bothering him, really, but one thing that stood out at the moment.

Finally, he couldn't keep it in any longer and blurted out, "Why did Adam make us leave?"

Sophia stirred. She'd been sitting on one of the couches, staring off into the distance at nothing. "What? He didn't *make* us."

"Maybe not," Grayson said. "But he made it clear that he didn't want us there anymore. And he knew that Bowltre would be waiting for us! So why didn't he tell us to stay there, where it was safe?"

The more he spoke, the angrier Grayson got. Adam was an adult! One of only two who even knew the kids were around. Why wasn't he helping them more?

"Adam's just Adam," Caleb shrugged. "He does the things he does. We have a safe-place with him, but we can't stay there all the time."

"Why not?" Grayson demanded.

"It's just… the way he is," Caleb said again, but more slowly this time, as if he really wasn't sure what he was trying to say.

"Pfft." Jonah scoffed and sat up. He'd been lying on the floor, staring at the ceiling. "I told you he was weird. And I didn't just mean his legs."

"That's not really fair, Jonah," Sophia said. "Adam is okay. He's just—"

He's not. Not really.

The wand spoke inside Grayson's head.

"What are you talking about?" Grayson asked out loud.

The wand didn't answer, but his friends all looked at him as if he'd lost his mind.

"The wand started telling me something," Grayson explained. "But now it's stopped."

My words are for you alone, the wand said.

"No. No more secrets." Grayson looked around at everyone. "We're all in this together. We have to work as a team. If you're part of it, great. If not, I'll give you to Jonah or throw you away."

Caleb's eyebrows rose at the harshness of Grayson's voice, but he didn't say anything.

For a moment, the wand remained silent, but then it finally spoke again.

All right. Then know that Adam's mind is broken, too. Not as severely as Nicholas Bowltre's is, but it is nevertheless. It is an effect of keeping a wand too long, regardless of his good intentions. When you are all with him, with your other wands, it begins to affect him even more. That is why after an amount of time has passed, he seems to act strangely.

When it finished speaking to him, Grayson told his friends what it had said, and continued passing on the wand's answers to their questions.

"Poor Adam," Sam said. "I had no idea."

"None of us did," Caleb said. "But I still don't understand. If having wands all gathered in one place causes bad things, why isn't it happening to us?"

Grayson waited. "Well?" he finally said.

You are not adults. As long as you only hold one wand at a time, you are free to be together. Adam is an adult, and holding a wand this long has opened his mind to influences that would not bother you.

"And since Bowltre is actually holding a lot of them, all the time, it's much worse with him," Grayson said. "I'm right, aren't I?"

You are. Nicholas Bowltre holds six wands. Four of which you are already aware. Two of which you are not, although you've seen their effects.

Grayson again relayed this to everyone else.

"We know he has Pete," Jonah scowled.

"We'll get it back," Caleb assured him. "The lightning wand is another."

"And one that lets him change into a dog. Maybe other things, too," Grayson said. "I saw him use it."

"And one that makes him invisible. So what are the other two?" Sophia asked.

Sam spoke up before the wand answered. "The fifth must be the one that makes our parents and everyone else forget us. How else would he be doing that?"

Exactly, the wand said in Grayson's mind.

"Then there's still a sixth," he said. "What is that one?"

That one is why I had you wait. I was trying to communicate with the others, to discover which of us Nicholas held. I was being blocked in my efforts, however.

"By what?" Caleb asked, after Grayson had passed on the wand's answer.

By my counterpart, the wand said.

"What's that mean?" Jonah asked.

Grayson thought he had an idea and the very thought made him feel cold all over.

"It's a wand that makes Bowltre's wands stronger, isn't it?" he said quietly.

It is. Very good, Grayson.

"You can do the same," Caleb said. "That's why Sam could pull Jonah away from Bowltre. And why I could make such a big crack in the street and Sophia could hide all of us."

The wand didn't reply for a moment, then it said, *Yes, in a way.*

Grayson waited, but it didn't say anything more.

"Are you going to tell us how that is?" he asked after a few moments had passed.

The wand stayed silent.

Grayson sighed. "Sorry guys. I guess it's done talking and has told us everything it wants to for now."

"Can't you make it?" Sophia asked.

Grayson shrugged. "I don't think so. I don't know how to, anyway. It's not like I've ever even really used it to make magic, like you guys. I've just kind of carried it around."

"Maybe," Caleb said. "I think there's more to it than that, though. And if it doesn't want to tell us, I know where we might be able to find out."

"The book" Sam said.

"The book," Caleb agreed.

"I couldn't read a word of it, though," Grayson said. "It's written in really weird letters."

"I know, that's why I had it. I was practicing with it. Besides, I don't really have to read it, Adam can. By tomorrow, he'll be better again, so we can go and explain what we're looking for."

"Maybe not everyone, though," Grayson said. "If being around the wands does bother him, it would probably be better if we weren't all there."

"I'll stay away," Jonah said. "No problem there."

"Me too," Sam said. "I've got some other things I can do."

"I want to go," Sophia said.

It was back to the three of them, Grayson thought. Just like it had started for him.

Chapter 34

A bright and sunny sky greeted them when they cautiously opened the cellar doors the next morning.

"If he's there, blast a crack open right under him again," Sophia hissed.

She was standing behind Caleb, her own wand at the ready.

Grayson didn't think Mr. Bowltre was around. His stomach felt fine, he had no urge to hide, and his wand hadn't said a word.

"It's safe. I think," he said. Although, as he said it, it occurred to him that Mr. Bowltre seemed to have come up with a new way to hide from Grayson's wand.

Before he could take back what he said, though, Caleb climber out and looked around. "Unless he's invisible, he's not here."

Sophia and Grayson followed him, their heads swiveling to try to look in every direction at once.

There was nothing to be heard but the normal sounds of any neighborhood. A couple of lawn mowers were buzzing away and somewhere a dog barked. A car went by on the street without the driver ever noticing them.

It could be a nice neighborhood, Grayson thought, if it weren't for the wands and the trouble they'd brought.

He half-expected his own wand to protest at that thought, but it remained silent as it had for the rest of last night.

Grayson looked down the street. There were no obvious threats, but somehow it seemed like a very long journey to get to the safety of Adam's house.

"No sense in just standing here," Sophia said. "Let's go find out what we need to. Unless your wand wants to just start talking again?"

They waited, but the wand said nothing. Finally, Grayson grimaced and said, "Nothing. Let's just go."

His heart pounded hard in his chest for the entire walk. Every time he heard anything, he jumped, sure that it was Mr. Bowltre coming for them.

"Should I hide us?" Sophia finally asked.

"No," Caleb answered. "Not unless we need you to. Remember how much it wiped you out?"

Sophia scowled. "I can take it."

"I know," Caleb said easily. "But it'd be better if you were fresh when we really need it. What if he comes after us on our way back?"

Sophia didn't answer, but Grayson could see that Caleb's reasoning made sense to her.

They all kept their wands at the ready, though, even Grayson, who didn't have to. His was the only one they knew of that worked all the time, without him needing to hold onto it.

Finally, after what seemed like forever, they reached Adam's house.

Grayson breathed a sigh of relief and started across the street, but Caleb put his arm out and stopped him.

"There's something wrong," he said. "Look."

He pointed at the low, iron gate, which was wide open. There were scorch marks on the pavement underneath, but Grayson couldn't remember if those had been there from when Mr. Bowltre had gotten blasted the day before.

"Maybe Adam went out," Grayson said.

Sophia shook her head. "He never does. His legs, remember? Adults see him, so he wouldn't take that chance."

"Careful," Caleb said and led the way slowly across the street.

When they neared, Grayson could see that the front door was ajar, as well. As a matter of fact, it was now hanging at an angle, suspended by only one hinge.

"This isn't good," Sophia whispered. "Maybe we shouldn't—"

"We have to," Grayson said. "What if he's hurt? Or needs our help?"

He could imagine Adam having tipped out of his chair; the wood of his legs having grown farther up so that he could no longer bend his knees. He might have been lying helpless all night.

"Adam?" he called. "It's us. Are you all right?"

Nobody answered.

The three looked at each other, then mounted the steps. Caleb poked his head inside the ruined door and called again.

Again, no answer.

Finally, they entered, wands at the ready.

The house looked like a cyclone had come through. The stacks of books, papers, and other items had been scattered everywhere. Several of the books had pages ripped from their spines and shattered glass littered the floor.

The round, lower tower room was no different. Books had been torn from shelves and destroyed. The furniture had been shredded by what looked like gigantic claws. Scorch marks stained the walls and the floor.

"Adam!" Sophia yelled.

They searched the entire lower level, finding the same disorder everywhere.

But there was no sign of Adam at all.

Chapter 35

"Bowltre must have gotten in." Caleb scowled as the three returned to the tower room. "But how?"

"Because of that wand," Grayson answered. "It's not just making his other *wands* stronger, it seems to be making him stronger, too. Remember how he almost got in yesterday? The only reason he didn't is because I was here with my wand, and that helped stop him. Without us…" He looked down.

"Where's the book?" Sophia asked. She was standing behind the mess on Adam's desk and moving things around. "It's not here."

"Maybe he put in on one of the shelves," Caleb said.

After searching every shelf and looking in every stack, they were finally forced to conclude that Mr. Bowltre had not only taken Adam, but the book as well.

"Why didn't he just take Adam's wand, though?" Sophia asked. "Why did he take Adam?"

Grayson's stomach tied itself into a knot. "Maybe he didn't." He swallowed hard. "Maybe he just… killed him."

"No." Caleb's voice was determined. "If that was true, his body would still be here. Why would Bowltre take it? He didn't kill Adam; he took him somewhere."

Grayson wasn't going to argue. He hoped very much that Caleb was right, and he hadn't known the man nearly as long as Caleb. What had Adam said? Caleb was the first one he saw being chased by Mr. Bowltre, so he knew that he needed to continue what he was doing.

Grayson plopped down heavily in a cleared chair. Adam had tried to give them all a safe place, including the wands. He'd given up his own health and risked his own life for them. Now, it looked like he was paying the price for his kindness.

They had to find him. Then, they had to get Pete back for Jonah. Then, they had to find out how to make their parents remember them all.

His head was down and he was staring at the floor, but that didn't stop Sophia from hearing the quick chuckle that escaped him.

"What's so funny?" she demanded.

"This," Grayson replied, looking up at her. "This whole thing. First, it was make our parents remember us. Then it was rescue Pete. Now, it's rescue Adam. What's next? We have to find a kitten that flew to the moon?" He laughed again.

The other two were staring at him.

"Are you all right?" Caleb finally asked.

"I'm fine," Grayson answered. "It's just... I don't know. I didn't mean to laugh. None of this is funny. It's just..."

"Too much," Sophia unexpectedly continued when he trailed off. "You're right. It's one thing after another. How are we supposed to deal with it all?"

Grayson looked at her gratefully.

"That may be," Caleb said. "But it doesn't change things. If *we* don't do it, who will? And what's our alternative? Leave Adam to Bowltre? Go through the rest of our lives without our parents knowing who we are? What happens when we become adults?"

"Maybe we forget ourselves," Sophia said. "We'll just wander around and bump into things because we don't remember that we're there!"

She snickered and quickly covered her mouth with one hand.

"Yeah," Grayson said. "We'll fart and then look around wondering who did it!"

Sophia laughed harder and Caleb grinned.

"Gross. I wonder if we'll ever think to look in the mirror?" he said. "Maybe we'll never wash and just walk around dirty all the time. We'll go by someone and they'll wonder where the horrible stink is coming from."

"Especially if we fart!" Sophia cried and all three almost collapsed with laughter.

I don't understand why any of that is funny, Grayson's wand suddenly said.

For some reason, that struck Grayson as even funnier, and he laughed even harder.

Chapter 36

Eventually, their laughter died down, and the seriousness of what they had discovered sunk in again.

"What are we going to do?" Sophia asked. "We don't have a safe space anymore, and Bowltre knows where our clubhouse is."

"I don't know." Caleb shook his head, then turned to Grayson. "What do you think?"

Caleb's question took Grayson by surprise. Caleb was the leader of their little group, so why was he asking Grayson what to do?

A good leader puts everyone's abilities to the best use, the wand said. *Caleb knows that, even if he doesn't realize that he knows it.*

"Oh, so you are still there," Grayson said inside his head. "What happened here?"

Exactly what you suspect. Nicholas Bowltre was here, with his wands.

"And Adam?" Grayson asked. "What happened to him?"

That I don't know. I can tell you, however, that he is not in this house, nor is his wand. But where they are, I have no idea.

"What should we do?" Grayson really wanted someone else to answer Caleb's question to him, but the wand fell silent once again.

He sighed. "I don't know," he finally said aloud. "I guess we should go back and let Sam and Jonah know what's happened. Then... maybe find a place for a new clubhouse?"

"Maybe," Caleb said. "You're both right that it's not safe anymore. But I'm getting sick of just running back and forth between here and there, dodging Bowltre every time."

"Me, too," Sophia said. "But what choice do we have?"

Caleb didn't say anything. After a few moments, he sighed and started to pace around the room. "I don't know," he said. "I just know I'm tired of it."

And suddenly, to Grayson's eyes, Caleb *did* look tired. Grayson remembered again that Adam had said Caleb was the first, and Sophia had told him that she'd moved to the town a couple of months ago. So... Caleb had been on his own for longer than that...

"Caleb," he said quietly. "How old are you?"

Caleb stopped pacing and looked at him. "Almost thirteen. Why? How old are you?"

"Eleven," Grayson answered. "And a half." He hesitated, then asked, "When did you find your wand?"

Caleb stared at him for a second. His look told Grayson that he knew what Grayson was really asking. "I was around your age," he finally said.

Grayson nodded. "And Bowltre showed up when?"

"A couple of months after that. It was only a few weeks after that when my mother and father started to forget me. That's what you're asking about, right? Only it wasn't as quick as with you. Maybe Bowltre was just learning how to use that wand or something."

So, Caleb found the wand at around eleven and a half years of age, he had it for a few months, and then a few more weeks before his parents forgot him. All of which meant that Caleb had been on his own, except for Adam, for almost a year. Unless Jonah or Sam were around, but still... Caleb had been essentially alone for a long time.

"I'm sorry," Grayson said quietly.

"Hey, don't worry about it." Caleb laughed, but it sounded forced. "I'm good. Hasn't been a problem for me."

"What are you guys talking about?" Sophia demanded.

"Nothing," Caleb said. "Nothing important anyway. What is important is that we figure out what to do next."

"You said you were tired," Grayson said.

"I am," Caleb replied. "But I still don't know what to do."

"We take the fight to Bowltre," Grayson said.

"I love it!" Sophia jumped up, then sagged a bit. "How?"

"I don't know, yet," Grayson said. "But Caleb is right. It's stupid to just keep going back and forth and running away from him. He's got a bunch of wands. So what? We know what a few of them do. The forgetting one can't hurt us. Neither can Pete. And the invisible one just lets him get close, but we can do the same thing with Sophia's wand. What does that leave?"

"The shape changing wand," Sophia said. "We'll see him use that, though."

"Right," Grayson agreed. "Although… we don't know that he can't use it on us."

"I don't think he can," Caleb said. "If he could have, why wouldn't he have changed me into something slow, like a turtle, when he was chasing me?"

"Good point." Grayson considered. "So that just leaves the lightning wand—"

"Which is enough," Sophia cut in.

"And the other master wand, thing," Caleb said.

The most dangerous, the wand told Grayson silently.

Grayson sat back in his chair and looked around, hoping to see something that would inspire some sort of idea in him. He saw nothing, though. It was just a big, old house, full of things from way back. That one shelf even held a bunch of kids' books that must have been Adam's when he was little and growing up there.

His eyes went back to those books. There was something there. Something that might be the answer.

Only, it wasn't the books.

"I have an idea," he told the others.

Chapter 37

"We need to find Bowltre's house," Grayson announced, his eyes still on the shelf of children's books.

Sophia and Caleb glanced at each other.

"Uhh. . .what makes you think he has one?" Sophia asked.

"He's an adult. Adults have houses. Even someone like Bowltre. And, I'll bet, just like Adam, it's the same house he grew up in."

"Why would that be?" Caleb asked.

"Just a feeling," Grayson replied. He nodded to the books he'd been looking at. "Adam keeps things like those books. And he's living in the same house his parents did. There are times when we've talked to him that he seemed almost like a kid himself. I don't think Bowltre is much different."

"Huh," Sophia said. "So does that mean we're all going to grow up and still be stuck like kids, too?"

"No," Caleb said. "It's happening to those two because they held onto their wands." He turned back to Grayson, visibly excited. "I'll bet you're right! Now all we have to do is find out where Bowltre came from!"

"Right," Grayson said. He sat back and waited.

Sophia and Caleb continued to look at him, but they didn't say anything else.

"What?" Grayson finally asked.

"Where do we go?" Sophia asked.

"I don't know! I'm not from here. You guys have been here a lot longer. Isn't there like some old house that kids won't go near, or that's all boarded up, or... I don't know. Like a haunted house?"

Caleb shook his head. "Not that I know of. But I never went all that far from my house before my parents forgot me... how about you?"

"Nope," Sophia said. "I never had the chance. Like Grayson, I found my wand pretty quickly after I got here."

"Then how do we find out where he might live?" Grayson asked.

No one had any idea, so they all sat and looked around, hoping that something would jump out at them and tell them what they wanted to know.

It didn't, and slowly, the gloom on Adam's vacant house started to settle in around Grayson. It felt heavy, like the air was too thick. The bright sunlight that came through the window was alive with tiny, sparkling dust motes, which made Grayson feel like he was inhaling a lungful of sandpaper every time he breathed in.

The ceiling suddenly felt lower and the walls closer together. He looked out the window at the sunny day and didn't want to be inside any longer.

Sophia and Caleb both seemed to be getting restless as well.

"I think we should—" Caleb began.

"Why don't we—" Grayson said at the same time.

"Let's go!" Sophia followed up, and without another word they almost ran from the house, but Grayson paused on the porch.

"What about the door?" It was still open, hanging from one hinge.

Caleb took it and pulled it shut as best he could, lifting it by the handle so it fit in the frame again. He stepped back and gazed at it.

"I hope he's okay," he said softly.

"Me, too," Grayson said.

They hurried off the porch and caught up with Sophia, who had already started down the block.

Back to the clubhouse, Grayson thought to himself. Maybe for the last time.

Chapter 38

The walk back was as uneventful as the trip to Adam's had been a short time before. Not only did Mr. Bowltre not make an appearance, but it didn't even feel as if he was anywhere around. In fact, if it hadn't been that they passed adults, both in cars and on the sidewalk, who didn't even see them, it would have been a perfect summer day.

Which made Grayson feel that something was horribly wrong, and, as they neared their destination, he began to think that maybe it was because Mr. Bowltre had already beaten them back to the clubhouse. He could imagine it torn up just as Adam's house had been.

He tried not to let his nervousness show, but he did quicken his pace a bit.

When they arrived, he hurried down the steps, sure by this point that he had been right.

Instead, all he found was Jonah, lying on one of the couches and reading a comic book. Sam wasn't present.

"You guys are back early," Jonah said. He didn't get up or even do more than glance at them. "How'd it go?"

"Not good," Caleb said.

Jonah snorted. "I'm not surprised. What happened? Did he get all weird again?"

Grayson sat down. "No. He didn't have the chance."

They told Jonah what they had found and what they suspected.

"Wow," Jonah said when they had finished. He paused, seemed to consider something and just said, "Wow," again.

"Yeah." Caleb got four bottles of Coke from the refrigerator and handed them around. "So now we need to figure out where Bowltre lives."

"How are we supposed to do that?" Jonah asked.

No one had any ideas.

"Maybe we can find one of the others that Adam told us about," Sophia suggested. "They would probably know."

"Except we don't even know who they are," Caleb said. "I don't even remember their names, do you?"

"Jerry and Abigail," Grayson said. "But we don't know their last names. As a matter of fact, what is *Adam's* last name?".

"I never asked," Caleb said. "That's kind of weird."

"So the only last name we know is Bowltre's," Sophia said. "Which doesn't help us at all."

"Of course it does," a new voice chimed in.

Sam came down the stairs and into the room with a book held in one hand. Everyone stopped and stared at her.

"Oh, for... haven't any of you guys ever heard of a library?" she asked. When no one answered her, she held up the book she carried. "Library? Where they have books? And computers? Where do you guys think I go all the time?"

Grayson looked at Caleb, who shrugged and turned to Sophia. She didn't even bother to look at Jonah.

Sam let the book fall to her side.

"Come on," she sighed. "We can use a computer there to hopefully look up his address. I heard you guys talking about needing to find where he lives. You can fill me in on the rest while we walk."

She turned and left the basement, followed by Jonah who jumped up and ran after her.

"The library." Caleb grinned at Grayson. "Why didn't you think of that?"

Grayson smiled back. "I was just going to say that when Sam came in."

"Yeah, well, let's just hope Bowltre doesn't like to read," Sophia said.

Chapter 39

"Why the library?" Grayson asked while walking next to Sam.

"It's quiet," she said. "And everyone kind of ignores everyone else there, anyway. They're all busy reading, or looking things up, or finding a book or movie. No one is really talking to anyone else. It makes me feel less strange."

Grayson nodded. He could understand that. When it was just him and his new friends, he felt fine. But every time they went out anywhere, every time an adult looked right through him, it reminded him of how strange and scary his life had become.

Maybe going to a place where everyone acted like that to everyone else wasn't a bad idea.

When they walked in, Grayson saw immediately what Sam meant.

It was the middle of the day, so there weren't many people present. There were no kids at all that Grayson could see. Only a few adults were browsing through the shelves of books or reading a newspaper or sitting at a computer terminal. Most of them were much older than Grayson's parents, but still, none of them even glanced at the kids as they came through the door.

Sophia made a bee-line for one of the computers, pulled out the chair and sat down at it. She began typing on the keyboard, her fingers moving faster than Grayson could follow. She didn't say anything, but her eyebrows drew down in a frown of concentration.

After a minute or two, he found his attention wandering. Whatever Sam was doing might have been important, but there was only so much watching someone else type that he could take. Instead, he looked around the room again.

It was the middle of the day. He recognized that, so it made sense that a lot of adults would be at work.

But adults didn't get summers off. Kids, however, *did* get them off from school.

So then, why were there *no* kids there?

Grayson had never been big on going to the library, but some kids liked it. Sam was one of those. Plus, didn't mothers sometimes bring their littler kids? And didn't most libraries have some sort of activity club for children during the summer?

Grayson strolled around, looking on the ends of the shelves and the bulletin board near the entrance.

None of the flyers or signs that were posted had anything to do with kids.

It all seemed very strange, even in the midst of everything else that was happening.

He found Caleb, who was by now ambling slowly down an aisle, trailing one hand lightly along the book spines.

"Where are all the kids?" Grayson asked.

He kept his voice hushed, even though he knew that no one, including the librarians, would have heard if he had spoken louder.

"What kids?" Caleb asked in an equally quiet voice.

"Any. Are we the only ones in this whole town? I haven't seen any but you and the others."

"Heh. No. Of course there are others. There's…" His voice trailed off as he considered. "I know there are. I think I remember them…"

Grayson looked around. "They're not here."

"No," Caleb agreed. "That *is* kind of weird, isn't it? Maybe we should—"

"Hey!" Jonah didn't have the same feeling about shouting in a library as Grayson did. "We found something!"

Just as Grayson had suspected, not a single adult even twitched at Jonah's outburst.

Sam was sitting back in her chair, the monitor glowing in front of her. When Grayson looked over her shoulder, he saw a picture of an old house, much like Adam's but even larger. It wasn't in very good shape, though. Some of the windows were busted and the paint was peeling. The yard was overgrown with weeds and a few dead trees. It looked to have been abandoned for years.

"So much for that," Sophia said. "I don't think a ghost would live there."

"Don't be so sure," Sam said.

She pointed and Grayson leaned forward to read what it said.

Above the picture in bold print read the words:

Bowltre estate saved from demolition by last minute purchase.

"This place was going to be torn down several years ago," Sam said. "The article says that someone bought it and paid the back taxes just in time."

"And then what?" Caleb asked.

"It doesn't say," Sam shrugged. "And this was the only thing I could really find on it."

"So close," Grayson said. "I just wish we knew where it was."

"We do," Sam said. "The address is in the article."

Chapter 40

The house still looked almost exactly like it had in the picture they all saw on the computer screen. It was a massive old place, with wood siding that was now gray with age and starting to fall off in places. The yard was even more overgrown now, to the point that it hid whole sections of the building. At one time, a walkway had led the way from the sidewalk to the front porch, but it was now cracked and pushed up in uneven slabs.

As far as the large, deep porch, it was falling apart, too, with rickety wooden steps that led to half-rotted boards. A heavy wooden door was the only thing about the whole place that still looked solid.

Around back, where a driveway once ran, was a large, detached garage. An older car was parked there, it's once red paint now mottled with rust.

"That must be the car that Adam had talked about. So Bowltre *is* here." Sophia's grip tightened on her wand.

"We don't really know that," Grayson said. "We don't know the last time he used it. Look at that thing. It probably doesn't even run anymore."

"Besides, we kind of figured he was here anyway," Caleb said. "And, if not, maybe we can get some ideas about how to beat him."

"If we can get inside," Sam said.

Between where they stood on the sidewalk and the house was a fence, also much like at Adam's, only this one was made of wooden pickets, most of which were by now rotted and falling apart.

"If he took Adam's wand," Jonah said, "like he took mine, then do you think he's using it to make a safe space for himself?"

"Good question," Grayson said. "There's only one way to find out."

Before any of the others could try to stop him, and before he changed his mind, Grayson stepped through the gap where a gate used to be. He held his breath, waiting for the same type of shock that Mr. Bowltre had gotten when he tried to get into Adam's.

That won't happen, his wand said. *That was only because he was fighting it.*

"So what would happen to me, then?" Grayson asked.

Nothing. You just wouldn't be able to move past a certain point. Nicholas didn't make a safe space, or, if he did, it doesn't extend this far.

Grayson turned to the others. "There's nothing here. We can go on."

But once they were all on the property, they still weren't sure what to do next. The door *was* solid, and the thought of trying to cross the large porch without falling through the boards didn't appeal to any of them.

"Back door," Caleb said. "This place is huge. There's probably several doors."

Walking through the yard was almost like trying to push through a jungle. Weeds grew up to their armpits and tangled around their legs. Briars were intertwined throughout and scratched them without warning.

Even more disturbing though, were the windows. They were so grimy that it was impossible to see through them, with even the little bit of sunlight that came through the mess of trees and vines, reflecting off the glass. Anyone on the inside though, could probably see them just fine.

"I can hide us," Sophia said quietly, but Caleb shook his head.

"No. It's better to save your strength. We don't know that he's even here. If we hear anything, or

Grayson says his wand is telling him something, we'll do it then."

Finally, they found their way to the rear of the house. All of them were dirty, itchy, and torn-up from the thorns. They panted for breath and scratched their welts, and their throats were dry from the heat and exertion.

"Wait," Sam said. "Before we do anything else."

She pulled her wand out, pointed it away from her, held her other hand outstretched and open, and concentrated. A moment later, a bottle of water appeared in her empty hand. She grabbed it, tossed it to Jonah and repeated the act four more times, until all had a chance to drink.

"Where'd they come from?" Grayson asked as he wiped his mouth on his sleeve.

"No idea. Some store or house over that way, I guess."

Grayson still wasn't overly comfortable with the idea of taking things that didn't belong to them, but she was right. They needed to have water, and it was either this way, or simply walk into someplace and take it. It was just one more thing that Mr. Bowltre's greed was forcing them to do.

"All right," Caleb said when he'd finished his bottle of water. "Let's do this."

Chapter 41

They did find a back door, but it was closed and as secure as the front had been. On the entire house, the doors were the only things that appeared to be taken care of. That would seem to mean that someone was living there, Grayson thought.

It didn't help give them any idea of how to get inside, though.

To make matters worse, it was starting to get late. They'd slept in that morning, after the ordeals of the night before. Then, the trip to Adam's house and the discovery of his disappearance had taken a few hours. Filling Jonah in on what they had found, going to the library, and searching for information had taken even more. And finally, the Bowltre estate, as the article had called it, was a good distance away from where they'd started.

Now, the light was getting that end of day quality. It wasn't going to be long before it was dark, and once that happened... Well, Grayson didn't think the place had lights.

"Spread out," Caleb said. "But no one goes in by themselves! If you find something, call out, quietly. We wait until we're all together to go inside."

Grayson headed toward the opposite side of the house from the direction they'd come in from. Maybe there was another side door that they could use or even a broken window.

He pushed his way through the overgrowth, keeping his eyes focused on the wall in front of him and shoving branches out of the way to see better.

He was just forcing his way through a particularly tangled bush when his foot hit something and he tripped, just as he had that day in the woods when he'd found his wand.

Only, this wasn't a wand.

Instead, it was a low triangular wall of concrete. It was attached to the foundation wall and sloped from there down to somewhere hidden by the weeds.

Where had he seen something like that before?

It suddenly came to him and he bent down and started tearing vines and branches away. Moments later he'd uncovered the edge of a rusted metal door.

Cellar stairs, just like those leading down to the clubhouse! And most houses, if they had a cellar, had inside stairs leading to it also. Or at least Grayson hoped this one did.

He pushed his way back around to the rear of the house.

"I found it," he called, keeping his voice low.

He wasn't sure that anyone had heard him, but a moment later, Caleb appeared from around the other corner. Sam and Sophia came back from the street, where they'd been looking for broken windows, and Jonah came out of the garage.

"What?" He answered Caleb's raised brows. "I was looking for a ladder in case they found a window."

"Oh. Good plan." Caleb smiled. "But we don't need one. Grayson found a way in."

Grayson led them to his discovery, and they began clearing the doors. It was hard work, and they kept stopping to listen for any sound of Mr. Bowltre's footsteps. He never appeared, though, and soon the doors were cleared enough that they could be opened.

But when they were, they found a heavy metal lock on these as well. If Mr. Bowltre *was* living there, he wasn't overlooking anything.

"Now what?" Grayson asked.

"You're forgetting," Caleb said. He drew his wand from his back pocket. "I can break anything."

"Why didn't you just break the front door, then," Jonah asked.

"Noise." Grayson answered before Caleb could. "If he did that, Bowltre would hear us for sure. I'm surprised he hasn't already."

"I don't think he's home," Sam said. "Maybe he's out looking for us."

That thought gave them all pause, as Caleb pointed his wand at the lock. For a moment, nothing happened, then there was a quiet *snap*, and the lock sprang open.

Caleb looked at his wand in mild surprise. "Huh. I wasn't sure that would work. I was trying to just barely break it, so it wouldn't make too much noise."

Control is one of the ways you get stronger, Grayson's wand told him. *Caleb is quite remarkable.*

Sophia grabbed one door and Grayson the other. They pulled at the same time and with a much-too-loud squeal of rusted metal, the doors opened. They let them flop to the sides and peered down the rickety stairs into the darkness below.

"Well, if Bowltre is here, he heard that for sure," Jonah said.

They waited, but there was still no sound of Mr. Bowltre approaching.

"Time to go then," Caleb said. "Everyone be careful and stay together."

He led the way down the steps and into the basement.

Chapter 42

They took the stairs one after the other, since they didn't trust them to hold more than one person's weight at a time.

When Grayson reached the bottom, he moved out of the way for Sam to come down and tried to look around.

The shadows hid almost everything, but he could make out shelves against the wall and heaps of abandoned stuff all over the place. It was going to be tricky walking around without tripping on something.

Then, there was a click and a single light bulb came on. Jonah was standing directly under it, the pull-string still in his hand, looking very pleased with himself.

"Should we close the doors?" Sophia asked.

Grayson hadn't even considered that. Close the doors? What if Mr. Bowltre came back and put a new lock on them? They'd be trapped!

Then again, if he came home and saw them open, and noticed the light was on, he'd know they were there for sure…

"Yes," Caleb said. He took a moment to answer, which made Grayson think the same thoughts were probably going through his mind. "Better to not shout out that we're here if we don't have to."

They kept their voices low in case Mr. Bowltre was home, but there was no way to hide the screech of the closing doors when Jonah ran back up the stairs and pulled them shut.

They froze, listening hard, but there was no sound of movement or voices from overhead. If Mr. Bowltre was around, he might have been sleeping. It was the only way he wouldn't have heard the doors.

"Look for stairs," Caleb whispered.

The basement of the house was huge and split into several rooms. The one they started in looked like it had been used to dump unwanted things for years. An old-fashioned baby carriage was tossed on its side in one corner, and a desk built for a child was thrown in another. There were broken and rusted tools littering the floor and the shelves were filled with dusty glass canisters, filled to various degrees with brown liquid.

A doorless opening led to another room, this one much larger and cleaner. It was still dusty and cobwebby, but the first room was obviously the junk room. This one had well-stored boxes and bins, some of which were neatly labeled. By the light that filtered out of the first room, Sam found a switch and light flooded this room from several overhead fluorescent bulbs.

Once they were on, the basement almost had a homey feel to it. Not that it was someplace they'd want to spend a great deal of time, but more like it was... familiar.

"We were right," Sophia said.

She indicated a set of stairs at the far end of the room. Nearby was an old washing machine and dryer, next to a deep sink. Judging by the dust and spiderwebs, they didn't look like they had been used in a long time.

"I can't see Bowltre doing his laundry," Jonah said. "What would he wear while he was?"

An image of Mr. Bowltre wearing shorts and a tee-shirt came to Grayson, and he had to stifle a sudden outburst of giggles. It wasn't all *that* funny, really, but the laughter wanted to burst out of him anyway.

Caleb smiled, too.

"I can't see him doing a lot of things," he said.

They made their way to the steps and stood as a group at the bottom. No one wanted to be the first to go up.

"How are we going to do this?" Sam asked. "If he's there, he's going to hear us for sure if we open that door."

Caleb turned to Sophia. "Now. You're up. Can you hide us all when we open the door and go through? At least until we know if he's there?"

Sophia set her jaw. "Yes. I can. I think."

She can, the wand said calmly. *We'll help her.*

Grayson put his hand on her shoulder. He used the other to take his wand out of his pocket. "I'll help," he said.

She nodded, took her own wand from her shirt, passed the string over her head, and closed her eyes.

"Okay," she said after a few seconds had passed. "I'm ready."

Grayson didn't feel any different this time, or at least, not like last time. There was no weird, disconnected-from-what-was-going-on-around-him feeling. As a matter of fact, he felt pretty good!

You're getting stronger, too, his wand said.

Caleb looked at them all one more time, then slowly started up the steps.

Chapter 43

When Caleb turned the knob and slowly pushed the door open, it hardly made a sound. A soft creak, which could easily be mistaken for an old house settling, was the only indication that anything had moved.

Grayson let out the breath he'd been holding and followed Sophia, staying close enough to keep his hand on her shoulder.

The stairs came out into an entry hall, another set of stairs above led to the second floor. On their left was the front entrance, across from them was a sitting room of some sort, and to their right, the hallway continued to the kitchen.

Jonah was the last one up. He shut the door behind him as carefully as Caleb had opened it, and then they all waited.

Nothing happened. There was no sudden shout, no sound of Mr. Bowltre's heavy footsteps, and no muttering voice.

"I don't think he's home," Caleb whispered. "You can let go now."

Sophia dropped her wand and Grayson removed his hand from her shoulder.

"Is he right?" he silently asked his wand. "Is Bowltre really not here?"

Not that I can tell. Although the other wand can mask its presence from me.

That wasn't very reassuring, but Grayson knew it was the best his wand could do. Until they figured out a way to get the Evil Master Wand— as he'd started to think of it— away from Mr. Bowltre, they were going to have to be very watchful.

"Should we spread out?" Sophia asked. "We can cover more of the house that way. Maybe find out what happened to Adam quicker."

"When is that ever a good idea?" Jonah scoffed. "Haven't you ever watched a scary movie? Everyone split up so the monster can pick us off one by one!"

"I don't know," Sam said. "I think Sophia might be right." She looked around and shivered. "I don't like this place. I want to leave as quickly as we can."

"Me, too," Grayson said. "But I don't think we should separate. If we stay together, Sophia can hide us and my wand can help make all of yours stronger."

That made it two for splitting up and two for staying together. As always, they looked to Caleb for the final say.

"We stick together," he said. "It's safer."

"Figures," snorted Sophia. "Boys stick together."

"Well, so did you and Sam," Jonah pointed out.

"Yeah," Sophia said. "Because we're the smart ones."

"Ha!" Jonah gave a sarcastic laugh and was about to say more when Caleb cut him off.

"Enough. Let's look around. If we get lucky, we'll find Adam and get him out of here. Even if it's without his wand, at least we can get him someplace safe."

Grayson didn't want to remind him that without Adam's wand, there was no place that was safe. They needed both of them.

"This way." Caleb started off down the corridor to the right, and, with one last longing look at the front door and freedom from Mr. Bowltre's creepy house, Grayson followed.

They walked to the kitchen, where they finally found the proof they'd been looking for that Mr. Bowltre did, indeed, live there. Open cans of food that were half-eaten had spoons still stuck in them. Food that should have been heated up, like beans and corn, had been eaten cold. A loaf of bread was left open on the counter, with several of the slices growing a furry coat of white and green mold. A few half-rotten apples were scattered on an old, scarred table.

"Ugh," Sam said. "Do you really think he eats like this?"

"He's crazy," Sophia said. "I don't know that he even thinks about it. It's like all he cares about is getting more wands."

A swinging door was closed at the other end of the kitchen.

Caleb led the way to it, pushed it open, froze, and then backed up rapidly, bumping into Sam who was right behind him.

"Ouch!" she squealed, but Caleb turned and put his hand over her mouth, his eyes opened as wide as Grayson had ever seen them.

"What's wrong?" he whispered.

Caleb slowly removed his hand and looked back over his shoulder at the door. He remained still for a moment, then turned back to them.

"There are people sitting in there," he whispered.

Chapter 44

Grayson didn't think it very likely that the people Caleb had seen wouldn't have noticed him opening the door and then letting it swing shut again.

He waited with the others, sure that at any moment, someone would come bursting through the door. At the very least, he expected to hear animated conversation from the other side, but there was nothing.

Finally, he couldn't take the waiting anymore.

He eased past Caleb and put his hand on the door.

"What are you doing?" Sophia hissed.

"Looking," Grayson replied and slowly pushed on the door.

As soon as he could see into the room, he froze as Caleb had.

There was a figure of a woman sitting in a chair at a large table. A plate, glass, and silverware were set before her.

She didn't say anything, nor did she turn to see who was holding the door open.

Grayson pushed the door a little farther.

In total, there were four people who sat around the table, all perfectly still, all with complete place settings in front of them. Grayson didn't know who they were, but none of them had the hunched-back or spiky hair that Mr. Bowltre did.

"Hello?" he said quietly.

He could hear someone behind him jump when he spoke, but he ignored them and kept his eyes glued on the people at the table.

Still, no one answered him or moved.

"I don't think they're real," Grayson said.

He pushed the door wide open so that it stayed against the wall. The others crowded behind him as he made his way into what was clearly a dining room.

When he'd inched closer to the first figure, he stopped suddenly and gasped.

It was actually a statue of a woman, made out of some type of white stone. She was very pretty, with long hair carved to appear loose down her back. She was wearing a dress and sat with her hands in her lap.

"Wow," Jonah said. "That's really good."

"What do you know about sculpture?" Sophia asked him.

"Nothing," Jonah said. "I just think it looks real."

The next figure was a man with a short beard. This one seemed to be formed out of solid glass. They could see the back of the chair he sat in through his suit coat. Unlike the calm demeanor of the woman, this man looked angry, like the sculptor had caught him in mid-shout.

"This is weird," Sam said. "What are they supposed to be?"

"I think that one is probably Jerry," Caleb said. He stood next to another figure and didn't look at them. "The stone one might be Abigail, and I don't know who the other one is."

"Why do you think that?" Sophia asked.

"Because this is Adam," Caleb answered sadly.

Grayson walked around the table to stand at his friend's side.

Adam, now made entirely of wood, was seated in the chair. His face was frozen into an expression of pleading, as if he had been begging his one-time friend to not do something.

"Look, though," Sam said.

Grayson looked to where she was pointing.

Adam's legs were just *legs*. The rough, tree-like stumps were gone. Now, Adam looked like everyone else.

"Is he dead?" Jonah asked.

Caleb whirled on him. "What do you think? Could you breathe if you were made out of wood? Do you think your heart would beat?"

Johan drew back from Caleb's angry outburst. "I'm sorry," he said. "I just wasn't thinking about—"

"That's your problem," Caleb spat. "You never think."

"Hey," Sophia said. "Don't take this out on him. He didn't do it."

Caleb glared at her, too, then seemed to deflate.

"I'm sorry," he whispered. He turned back to Adam. "I just—"

Grayson felt horrible for his friend.

"We'll figure this out," he said. "Somehow…"

Silence fell, until Sam cleared her throat and said, "This must be the fifth person. The one Adam didn't mention."

She looked like she might have been the wild-one of their group. Now, she looked like she was made of clay, baked hard until it was a dark red color. Her hair was in spikes like Mr. Bowltre's, although they had no way of knowing what color it had been. She wore ripped pants and a jacket, which was covered in patches and open over a t-shirt with some sort of design. Her face was set in a sneer, and even though she was made of clay, Grayson thought she looked like she was saying something very bad.

"I wonder what her name is?" Sam said. She was staring at the figure with a small smile.

Grayson was opening his mouth to say something, when a noise from outside cut him off.

Stomp, drag. Stomp...drag...stomp.

Chapter 45

"It's him," Sophia whispered.

The sound of Mr. Bowltre's approach was different than it usually was. Instead of the steady stomp of his heavy boot, followed by the drag of his bad leg, this was more hesitant. The stomp was less forceful and the drag was slower. Either Mr. Bowltre was hurt, or he was tired, or…

"He's picking his way across the porch," Grayson realized. "He knows which boards are rotten and which are safe."

As if to verify his words, the sound of the uneven footsteps stopped and was replaced by that of a key in a lock. Grayson peered through the archway that led from the dining room. Beyond was the sitting room they'd seen earlier and then…the front door.

Even as he looked, the door swung open and they could see Mr. Bowltre silhouetted against the moonlit sky.

He stomped inside the entryway and stopped. His head came up and he sniffed.

"Something…" he growled.

Grayson was sure they were caught, but even though he stood in the open, Mr. Bowltre didn't seem to see him. He sniffed again, snarled, moved farther inside and swung the door shut behind him.

Grayson looked over his shoulder. The others were huddled together and Sophia had her wand out and pointed straight up. Her eyes were closed and her arms trembled with strain. When he saw Grayson looking, Caleb motioned frantically for him to come closer.

When he did, Grayson felt a little better and noticed some of the tension leave Sophia. It had been much harder for her to hide him when he was separate from the group.

"Help her," he told his wand.

He felt it again, and this time, it was back to feeling like it had at first. Almost immediately, he could feel a pull, like something was trying to get rid of Sophia's magic.

Mr. Bowltre stomped his way through the sitting room and entered the dining room. He paused and looked around; his large eyes narrowed as much as they could. Finally, he seemed satisfied.

"Friends," he muttered. "Still here. Still visiting. Good."

He continued into the kitchen and didn't seem to notice that the door that had been closed was now open.

"Food," he said louder. "We'll have food. All of us will eat. And talk. Like we used to."

Mr. Bowltre kept up a running commentary while he clattered around the kitchen. He talked to the immobile figures seated around the table like they were old friends who were answering him. His words swung back and forth between the crazed mutterings they were used to and the almost normal conversation of a perfectly sane man.

"Remember when we took the car to the lake?" he asked at one point. His words were clear and his sentences were complete. "We caught a ton of fish, and then we cooked them over the fire that Junie's wand made. Delicious."

Then, without warning, his voice changed. "Don't call her Junie. No. June. Her name is June. Stupid!"

He hit himself hard on the head. Grayson flinched, but Mr. Bowltre didn't seem affected by his own blow.

A few minutes later he returned to the dining room with several open cans with spoons sticking out of them held in one arm, hugged against his chest. He approached Adam, passing within a hand's breadth of the kids and put one of the cans down in front of him.

"New guest eats first," he growled. He reached out and gently patted Adam on the cheek.

He gave a can to Abigail next and softly touched her shoulder, then to the other woman, who was apparently named June.

After he set the can down, he stared down at her for a moment, then softly said. "Sorry. It's June. Not Junie. I remember. Sorry."

He leaned over and kissed her cheek, then scurried away as fast as his leg would allow him to move.

"Here," he said to the Jerry statue as he set the second to last can down in front of him. "No complaining. Sick of it. Always bad. Never good."

Jerry was the only one he didn't try to touch. Instead, he moved back around to the other side of the table, pulled out a chair next to June and sat.

He held his open can between his hands and smiled at the statues. "Eat," he said, his voice once again perfectly clear. "It's nice to have you all with me again."

Mr. Bowltre blinked, then started to eat his cold beans with great relish.

Grayson watched the whole thing and a funny feeling began to form in his stomach. Mr. Bowltre was an evil, selfish man, who had ruined their lives.

So why did he find it so easy to feel so bad for the man?

Chapter 46

Grayson was starting to get really tired again. They watched as Mr. Bowltre did nothing but eat his beans and occasionally look around at his friends. A couple of times, he seemed to try to smile, which made his already bizarre face look even more strange. Then, his smile would falter and he would quickly look away, back to his can of beans.

"I don't think I can do this much longer," Sophia whispered.

As soon as she spoke, Mr. Bowltre's head came up with a snap. A low growl escaped his throat as he looked around the room.

Grayson was afraid to even breathe.

After a few long moments, Mr. Bowltre returned to eating.

Caleb motioned, and they began to shuffle together very slowly toward the sitting room, trying to be as quiet as they could.

They had almost made it when Mr. Bowltre suddenly stood up. He burped loudly, sneaked a glance at June, and snickered.

"Sorry," he mumbled. "Rude."

He lowered his gaze and moved around the table collecting the other cans. If he noticed that no one else had eaten, he didn't comment.

The kids kept moving, until they were completely in the sitting room and out of his way. Grayson kept his eyes locked on Mr. Bowltre, waiting for him to start sniffing.

Instead, he took the cans to the kitchen and disappeared from sight.

With a deep sigh, Sophia let go of the magic and they were all in sight again.

"Come on," Caleb breathed, and led the way toward the front door.

Once there, however, he didn't open it. He started up the stairs to the second floor.

"No!" Jonah whispered. "We need to get out of here."

Caleb shook his head. "We're not done. We haven't found a way to stop him or get Adam back. We can't leave yet!"

He didn't wait for a reply. With a careful, slow tread, he began up the stairs.

Sophia stared at Grayson. He shrugged and started after Caleb, and a moment later, the others followed.

It was all Grayson could do to not hurry, to not run up the steps as fast as he could and hide somewhere where Mr. Bowltre couldn't find him. It was even harder to not turn and run out the front door, which seemed to beckon him from the bottom of the stairs.

He heard the stomp, drag of Mr. Bowltre's footsteps, but he stopped in the dining room and began talking to the inanimate people he kept there. Grayson heard him mutter something about a game and how there was to be no cheating.

Good, he thought to himself. That would give them some time. If nothing else, it would help him— and, more importantly, Sophia— to rest for a little while and regain some of their strength.

When they reached the top of the stairs, they found a hallway that led off to their left, while there was a large door on their right.

Caleb looked around and shrugged, then turned to Grayson.

"What do you think?" he whispered.

"I think we should just get out of here," Grayson whispered back. "But, since we're here, let's try this door."

The knob turned easily and the door was quiet as they swung it open, revealing a huge bedroom. A massive bed took up space along one wall, with large windows on either side. There were several other pieces of furniture and a fireplace with long-dead ashes still inside and two comfortable chairs in front of it.

Other than being dusty and having the smell rooms get when they've been closed up for a long time, the bedroom was neat and clean.

"This isn't Bowltre's room," Sam said.

"How do you know that?" Jonah asked.

"It's too nice," she replied. "I'd bet this was his parents' room, I bet. And he wouldn't be staying in here. Besides, you saw the kitchen. If he came in here a lot, it would be more like that. But I think this place was like... off-limits to him, or something."

"Then we can hide here for now," Caleb said. "Until later, when he falls asleep. Then we can look around a little more and find whatever we need."

Grayson wasn't quite sure anymore *what* they needed to find. Something to fight Mr. Bowltre with, for sure, but what would that be? They'd already found Adam. And he was sure that Mr. Bowltre now held Adam's wand. As well as the ones the others had possessed.

"Hey," he silently said to his wand. "Are you there? You haven't said much since we came in."

When his wand answered, it sounded as if it came from far away. The voice was weak and hard to make out.

It's too much. There are too...

Whatever the wand was trying to say faded away so that Grayson couldn't hear it.

"Too what?" he asked. "What are you saying?"

But there was no answer. Which made Grayson wonder. . . if they needed his wand to make his friends' wands stronger, to stand-up to Mr. Bowltre, was it going to be able to help them?

Chapter 47

They left the door cracked with Jonah sitting close by so he could hear if Mr. Bowltre came near the stairs. If he did, Jonah would shut the door very softly and let the others know.

The rest of them explored the room. It was a much larger bedroom than any Grayson had ever seen. Not only was there the room where the bed was, but there was a massive closet with clothes still hanging inside. Dresses, skirts, shirts, pants, and shoes were hung from rods and folded on shelves in a dizzying array.

Next to that was a bathroom, with a large, claw-footed tub and a big shower, as well as two sinks and a toilet.

The Bowltre estate, the article on the computer had called it, and now Grayson understood why. Whoever Nicholas Bowltre had been, before the wands came into his life, he'd come from a family with a lot of money.

He wandered back out of the bathroom and approached the bed, wondering what had happened to Mr. Bowltre's parents. Were they dead? Or did he keep them somewhere, turned into something hard and stashed in another room? That thought brought a quick shudder up his spine.

On the bedside table was a framed photograph. Grayson picked it up and studied the three smiling faces that looked back at him.

A man and woman, around the same age as Grayson's own parents, he would have guessed, stood on either side of a boy who was probably a young teenager. The boy was a tall, straight, well-groomed young man, and he stood proudly with his parents.

"This was him, huh?" Grayson showed the picture to Caleb who was sprawled out on the bed.

"Doesn't look much like him," Caleb said.

Grayson looked closer. The boy did have very large eyes. Not abnormally so, but large enough that he could see them growing into the protruding orbs Mr. Bowltre had.

It may have been his imagination, but Grayson thought he could see things in the other boy's eyes. Things like greed, and selfishness, and maybe… a little bit of crazy.

He shook his head. It was just a photograph. There was nothing more to it than that, and he was just letting his imagination run away from him.

After another hour had passed, Grayson was beginning to think they'd made a huge mistake by staying in the house. Mr. Bowltre was still in the dining room, talking to his frozen friends while he "played" a game with them. Every now and then, he'd burst into a hiccupping, strangled sort of laugh, as if someone had told him a hilarious joke.

"Is he ever going to bed?" Sophia groaned.

She was now lying on the bed, where she'd actually fallen asleep for a little while. The others sat or lay crosswise in the chairs near the old fireplace or on the floor.

Grayson had been sitting against the wall, near Jonah, for the last half-hour. He kept trying to talk to his wand, but each time, if he heard anything at all, it was so faint and indistinct that he couldn't make out what it was saying.

He tried again.

"Where are you?" he asked silently.

A far-off buzzing was all the answer he got.

It had to have something to do with Mr. Bowltre. Before he'd come home, the wand was speaking to him fine. So why was it now—?

Stomp, drag. Stomp, drag.

Jonah's eyes grew wide, but he didn't move. He kept his stare focused on the door that he was supposed to close. The door that Mr. Bowltre would surely notice was cracked open.

Stomp, drag. Stomp, drag.

He was coming down the hallway from the kitchen, past the door to the basement.

Stomp, drag.

He was at the bottom of the stairs.

Stomp. Drag. Stomp.

He was on the lowest stairs.

Grayson eased past Jonah, who was trembling, and put his hand on the door.

For a moment, a bizarre desire to leave it open came over him. They could watch Mr. Bowltre limp up the stairs. They could sneak out and stand at the top, and when Bowltre lifted his head and saw them, it would be too late. They could shove him, and Caleb could break the handrail. That would be the end of Mr. Bowltre, or at the very least, he'd be too injured to stop them or to retaliate.

Grayson didn't need his stomach to hurt to know that wasn't the right thing to do.

He closed the door slowly and carefully, timing the click of the latch with one of Mr. Bowltre's heavy stomps.

Then he moved away from the door and backed toward the bed. He sat on the edge and looked at the picture on the table again.

He picked it up and sighed. The list kept getting longer, rather than shorter.

Yes, they had to do everything else that they'd already discussed: get their parents to remember them again, get Pete back for Jonah, rescue Adam, if he was still alive at all.

And now…

Grayson looked down at the smiling family.

Maybe they could fix Mr. Bowltre, as well.

Chapter 48

The sound of Mr. Bowltre's footsteps faded as he went past the closed doorway. They listened as a door was opened, then slammed shut, and then, silence.

"What do you think?" Sam whispered. "Can we go now?"

"Not yet." Caleb shook his head. "Let's make sure he falls asleep first."

"Then we'll go?" Jonah asked.

Caleb didn't answer, and Grayson knew what that meant. They still hadn't found anything that was going to help them beat Mr. Bowltre and save Adam. The other adults around the table, too, he supposed.

He realized that he'd come to think of Adam as still being alive. He had simply been changed to wood, just as the others had been changed to stone, glass, and clay. Grayson didn't know if the Change Wand he'd seen Mr. Bowltre use to shift into a dog was what had been used, or if it was a different one, but it didn't really matter. The end result was still the same.

What was more, he knew that Caleb had convinced himself of the same thing. That was why he didn't answer Jonah. It wasn't really about beating Mr. Bowltre anymore. It was about saving Adam.

They resumed waiting until another half-hour had passed. Then, Caleb carefully opened the door a tiny crack and peered out.

From behind the closed door at the other end of the hallway, a new sound was shattering the otherwise silent large house.

Mr. Bowltre snored! And loudly!

A rasping, buzz-saw noise filled the hallway, loud enough that Grayson thought they could have run down the stairs without trying to be quiet at all, and Mr. Bowltre never would have heard them.

Caleb slipped out of the door and paused. Jonah followed, started down the top step, then turned and looked at the other boy.

"What are we waiting for?" he whispered.

Caleb motioned them all to draw near. When they had put their heads together, he said. "You guys go on. I'm going to see if there's anything up here that we can use to save Adam."

That confirmed what Grayson had suspected, and if Caleb had come to the same conclusion he had, then he also realized there was probably only one way to turn Adam back.

They needed to get the wand that had been used to make Adam and the others statues.

"I'm staying with you," Grayson whispered. "We can both look. The others can go open the door and get ready to run."

For a moment, it looked like Sophia was going to argue, but then she scowled, nodded, and followed Jonah and Sam down the stairs.

Caleb watched them go and then turned to Grayson.

"Thanks. Any idea what to do next?"

"Look around," Grayson shrugged. "But I think we both know where we're going to end up."

They looked to the end of the hall at the door where the snores were coming from.

"Might as well see what we see though," Caleb grinned.

Grayson smiled back, but his heart wasn't really in it. Caleb may have found this whole thing exciting, but for Grayson it was terrifying. Still, he couldn't leave his friend to face whatever was going to happen alone.

One by one, they cautiously opened the other doors. Two more bedrooms and another bathroom, plus a closet stuffed with towels and bedsheets were all they found.

Finally, the only thing left was Mr. Bowltre's room.

Before they opened that door, Grayson tried again to talk to his wand, but it still didn't respond. They were on their own.

He motioned for Caleb to follow him back toward the stairs. Once there, he whispered. "Let me go in."

"Why?" Caleb asked.

"Because your wand still works." He told Caleb what he'd discovered with his. "So you can watch Bowltre while I look around. If he wakes up, break his bed, or the floor, or something. Anything to give me time to run away."

"All right," Caleb nodded. "Makes sense. You sure you're up for it?"

No, Grayson wanted to say, but it really did seem like the best plan. "Yeah," he said instead. "Just keep an eye on him, okay?"

Caleb looked at him seriously. "Of course."

"Okay, then." Grayson swallowed hard and returned to Mr. Bowltre's bedroom door.

He drew his breath in, put his hand out, and twisted the handle. It turned easily, and the door opened.

Chapter 49

Mr. Bowltre's bed was a tangle of covers, so thick that Grayson couldn't even see him. They were heaped up around him in a mass that hid everything except, upon closer inspection, the points of his hair. But the loud snores coming from the pile told Grayson that he was still sound asleep.

Grayson peered around the room before he entered. Like every other room in the house, this one was huge. The bed was large and solid looking, and there was a dresser with pulled-out drawers and clothes hanging out of them. Shelves lined one wall, filled with old trophies, games, and books, while a messy desk was against another wall.

Clothes, dishes, and other things were tossed randomly around the floor, which made it difficult for Grayson to pick his way through without stepping on something that could break or trip him up. He was reminded of the room in the basement. Both were a stark contrast to the neatness of Mr. Bowltre's parents' room.

Near the bed was a chair, and on that chair were more clothes, including a long, dirty black coat. Heavy boots lay nearby.

Unless he kept them somewhere else when he was sleeping, the wands must still be in Mr. Bowltre's coat, Grayson thought. He looked to Caleb and pointed at the chair. Caleb nodded, lifted his wand, and held it steady, aimed directly at Mr. Bowltre.

Grayson moved slower than he ever had in his life. He took each step carefully, choosing where he was going to put his foot before he actually moved it. It took forever— more than forever— to get to the chair. Once, Mr. Bowltre stopped snoring and Grayson froze with one foot in the air. Bowltre growled, muttered something, tossed off a blanket as he flipped onto his other side, and promptly began snoring again. Grayson let out his breath and continued toward the coat.

Finally, he was there. He twitched it open so that he could see the inside. The one side flopped back with a soft clink.

They had been right! The wands *were* all there! There were six of them— no wait… there were more than that!

Grayson carefully lifted the other side, only to reveal even more wands.

His wand had been mistaken! Or maybe that was all Mr. Bowltre had on him the other day. Either way, he possessed many more wands than they'd thought.

Taking the Change Wand wasn't going to be enough. They didn't know what else he could do. Grayson knew that if Mr. Bowltre woke up and found the Change Wand gone, he'd realize what had happened. He'd come after them again, this time with wands that could do. . . well, who knew *what* they could do?

He needed to take the whole coat. Or would that only make things worse?

"Are you there?" He tried to ask his wand if he was doing the right thing, but it still either wouldn't, or couldn't, talk to him. Grayson wasn't even hearing a faint buzz now. There was only silence.

He had to make the decision on his own.

Grayson glanced back to make sure Caleb was still with him. He was, his eyes intent on the bed, but flickering every few seconds to Grayson.

Taking a deep breath, Grayson reached out and grabbed the coat.

Instantly, the world seemed to go berserk.

A huge spike of pain shot into Grayson's head, so bad that he reeled back, tripping over a plate that had been left on the floor. He stumbled backward, clutching the coat tightly to his chest.

Mr. Bowltre bolted upright on his bed and let loose with the loudest howl Grayson had ever heard. It drowned out every other noise. Grayson watched in horror as Mr. Bowltre turned toward him, stopping his howl but growling like a mad dog.

He lifted his hand and Grayson saw the wand he held.

No. That was wrong. He didn't hold it; it was part of him. It was as if the wand was fused into his left hand, becoming part of him.

Grayson couldn't move. The sight of Mr. Bowltre's hand and the pain in his head immobilized him. Mr. Bowltre snarled and started to push himself to the side of the bed.

"Thief! Wicked! Thief!"

He seemed incapable of saying anything more coherent. But it was enough. Their plan had failed.

A monstrous crack split the air, and Mr. Bowltre's bed collapsed in the middle, dragging both him and his covers inward, so that he was struggling to get untangled.

He struggled and howled, and the pain roared through Grayson's head again.

Suddenly, his wand was there.

"RUN!"

It was the only time Grayson had ever heard it be anything but perfectly calm. It shouted that one word in his mind, then was gone again.

Grayson felt like he could barely think. He took another faltering step backwards, spots dancing in front of his eyes, and tripped.

But before he could fall, Caleb grabbed him and pulled him toward the door.

"Let's go!" he cried.

He yanked Grayson from the room, slammed the door, and they ran toward the stairs. The pain in Grayson's head began to ease, a bit more with each step he took away from Mr. Bowltre.

Behind them, the bedroom door flew open, and Mr. Bowltre howled again.

Chapter 50

"Hurry!" Caleb yelled.

Grayson didn't need the encouragement. He glanced back one time, and that was enough.

Mr. Bowltre was running at them as fast as his damaged leg would allow him to move.

Without his coat and boats, Grayson could see what was wrong with him. Just like Adam, Mr. Bowltre's right leg was wooden. His was like a carved limb, with a fully formed foot, only, it didn't bend—not at the ankle and not at the knee. Grayson suspected that his change went all the way up his leg, which explained why Mr. Bowltre could only drag it along.

Regardless, he was moving faster than Grayson would have thought possible. He raised his hand again, and again, Grayson saw the Evil Master Wand fused into his hand. At the end of Mr. Bowltre's left arm his hand was gone. Now there was just a lump of flesh-colored skin, with the wooden wand sticking out of it.

"Hurry!' Caleb yelled again, and Grayson spun back around.

Caleb was gone! They hadn't reached the stairs yet, but his friend had vanished!

Then, just as suddenly, he was there again, running as fast as he could. He flickered out of sight once more just as he reached the top of the stairs and leapt down them.

Grayson was right on his heels. He flew onto the stairs and tried to jump, intending to take them three or four at a time. Only, when he did, his legs didn't work right and a searing pain shot up them.

Instead of jumping, his legs froze and he over-balanced, his arms windmilling. He had time to glance down and saw that his legs were fusing together, just as Mr. Bowltre's hand had fused with the wand. It felt like fire was licking at the insides of his legs, as if they were melting together.

Then, he lost his balance completely and crashed down the steps. He collided with Caleb near the bottom, although he still couldn't see him.

Hands grabbed him and dragged him to his feet.

"Are you all right?" Sophia cried.

Grayson nodded, although he was not at all sure if he was okay, but it didn't matter. They had to get out of there. Whatever Mr. Bowltre was doing, it was like he still had the wands.

"Oh no!"

Grayson's head snapped around at Jonah's cry. He was beginning to turn into black stone, starting with the tips of his fingers.

Next to him, Sam looked around wildly as light, puffy clouds began to surround her. If they kept gathering, she'd be blinded to anything else.

And Sophia suddenly let go of Grayson and stared around blankly as if she couldn't remember where she was or what she had been doing.

The door was *right there*! It was open and all they needed to do was get out, across the porch, and run away.

Above them, Mr. Bowltre growled from the top of the stairs.

"Mine! All mine! Thieves!" His shouts sounded like the barking of a dog. He was using his wand like a conductor's baton, and suddenly Grayson knew what he was doing.

The Evil Master Wand was controlling the others, even at a distance. Mr. Bowltre had used them so much that he could make them work, at least with the help of that wand, without holding them!

"The coat!" He yelped as more pain flared up. "He's using the wands in the coat!"

Sam stepped forward, out of the clouds building up around her, and pointed her own wand at Mr.

Bowltre's coat, which was puddled on the floor near Grayson.

A wand flew from the coat to her hand. She screamed briefly, then turned and threw it directly to Jonah, who caught it just as his hand was turning to stone.

"Pete!" he cried happily.

Then, with determination written all over his normally placid face, he faced Mr. Bowltre and used Pete.

Clouds: heavy, dark, dense clouds spilled out of the wand, sped up the stairs, and surrounded the hunchbacked man. Jonah gestured with Pete and the clouds began to swirl, faster and faster, and he added more of them, until Mr. Bowltre was lost to sight.

The pain in Grayson's legs began to fade and Caleb reappeared, patting at himself like he couldn't believe he was there.

Sophia grabbed Grayson again and pulled him to his feet fully this time. He stumbled momentarily, then bent and grabbed the coat, and they took off.

They leapt over the rotting boards on the porch, hoping they'd make it. A few broke, but they were running so fast that they managed to skip over them.

Moments later they were on the street and running as fast as if rabid dogs were chasing them.

Behind them, from inside the house, came another howl. Only this one, Grayson thought, sounded different.

This one sounded like it was full of pain and sadness, rather than rage.

Chapter 51

Hold onto that coat.

For the first time since entering Mr. Bowltre's house, Grayson could hear his wand clearly.

"I'm going to," he said.

They ran toward the clubhouse for several blocks, then had to slow down and catch their breath. Sophia had her wand at the ready, in case she needed to hide them, but no one saw or heard Mr. Bowltre approaching.

"I broke the staircase," Caleb panted. "Right before we ran. I don't think it will stop him, but it will give us some time."

"Good thinking," Jonah said. "I didn't even see you do it."

Caleb nodded. "Good job with the clouds, too. Remind me not to tease you about what Pete can do anymore."

Jonah looked very pleased with himself, but Sophia turned to Sam. "Why did you scream?"

"It hurt," she replied. "When I grabbed Jonah's wand. It felt like it was on fire or something."

She already held one. You cannot hold more than one wand at once without experiencing great pain.

Grayson told the others what his wand had said, as they continued walking toward Sophia's house.

"But how can Bowltre do it, then?" Sophia asked.

He doesn't. You have always only seen him use one wand at a time. But if he has at other times, I'm sure it hurt him a great deal.

The wand's answer just proved to Grayson, all over again, how crazy Mr. Bowltre really was. But a thought occurred to him, so he asked, "What about what he was doing? Right before we got away. How was he using all those wands at once, and without touching them?"

Grayson's wand took a few moments to reply. When it did, it sounded almost reluctant.

He wasn't using them. The wand he held was. As I've told you, that wand is like my… opposite, if you will. It can control other wands. It was making the wands in the coat use their magic against you.

"So… can you do the same thing?" Grayson asked. He kept that question silent, not sure how his friends would feel if they knew his wand could take control of theirs.

Not exactly. Where that one demands, I ask. I encourage. I… try to persuade.

That sounded evasive to Grayson, like the wand wasn't being completely honest.

"So you can, though. If asking doesn't work, you can force them to do something," he said.

The wand didn't answer.

Soon, they began to jog again, until they had finally made it back to Sophia's and the relative safety of the clubhouse.

Grayson would have loved nothing more than to lie down and go right to sleep, but there wasn't time for that. Now that they were safe, they had to decide what to do next. They had the wands. Given enough time, they could figure out which one was making their parents forget them and undo that magic.

But they didn't have that much time. Mr. Bowltre wasn't going to leave them alone. And Adam and his friends were still trapped in his house.

"We need to go back," Caleb said. "It's as simple as that. We take the Change Wand so we can free Adam but leave the other wands here. That way, Mr. Bowltre can't use them against us."

Knowing what he did about the one wand Mr. Bowltre did have left, Grayson was afraid that wouldn't be enough. He could change them all to stone or glass before they could do anything to stop him.

He took a deep breath and told his friends what his wand had told him.

"Oh." Caleb frowned for a moment, then smiled. "That's great!"

"It is?" Grayson had been waiting for them all to be angry about the news.

"Sure," Caleb said. "That means *your* wand can stop him from taking over the Change Wand. Right?"

"Is he right?" Caleb asked silently.

Yeeesss, his wand answered slowly. *In theory. Although it's not that simple. Nicholas Bowltre had a connection to the wands he's been using, as each of you do to your own. That's why Sam was able to pull Jonah's wand free but had not been able to take the Lightning Wand from Nicholas earlier. I can at least slow down his control of the Change Wand, but I can't guarantee I can stop him for long.*

"We don't have to worry about that, though," Sam said. "We can leave the Change Wand here and I'll bring it to us when we're ready for it."

"Of course!" Caleb agreed. "I should have thought of that. So, we'll leave in the morning. But for now…Sam, would you come outside with me? There's something I want to practice."

Sam nodded and the two started toward the stairs.

"Wait," Grayson said. "What is it?"

Caleb grinned at him. "You'll see," he said. "You're not the only one with ideas."

Chapter 52

They were quiet as they made their way back to the Bowltre estate early the next morning. All of them were tired and scared, but they knew that now was their best chance of finally beating Mr. Bowltre.

While they walked, Grayson's wand told him one more thing.

Nicholas Bowltre's mind is broken, it said.

"We already knew that," Grayson replied silently.

Yes. But it's worse now. My counterpart, that which you call the Evil Master Wand, is hurting him even more. If you truly wish to help him, you must get it away from him.

Grayson tried to hide his surprise. He hadn't told anyone his thought that maybe they could help save Mr. Bowltre, too.

You're a good kid, the wand said. *It's not surprising that you'd want to help him. But be careful, my counterpart could have yet another trick in store.*

Grayson kept what the wand had told him to himself. They all already knew to be careful around Mr. Bowltre. That wasn't anything new.

When they approached the house, it was the same as they had seen it last night, except the door that they had left open in their haste to escape had been closed again.

"Front door?" Caleb asked.

"Might as well," Sophia said. "We're not trying to hide from him this time. Besides, he doesn't have his wands. What can he do?"

"He still has one," Grayson said. "It's gross. Like it's part of his hand now. But it's dangerous."

"I thought that one was like yours?" Caleb said. "Like it can make other wands stronger or something."

"It's evil." Grayson shuddered. "I think it takes over other wands. Let's all be careful with ours."

"Always," Caleb grinned. "Besides, we're not going to give him a chance."

"Actually…" Grayson paused. "I want to speak to him first. Before we do anything else."

The rest looked at him as if he was crazy. He felt his cheeks burn but pressed ahead anyway.

"He needs help. He's… I don't know… sick or something. And the wand he has left is making it worse. If he gives it up, he maybe he'll get better."

Caleb stared at him for a second. "And you think you can convince him?"

"I don't know." Grayson shrugged. "I just think I should try."

I don't think—the wand began.

"I'm doing it," Grayson replied silently.

"Okay, then," Caleb agreed. "But we're all right here if it doesn't work."

Grayson nodded, walked up the steps and picked his way carefully across the rotting porch. He stopped at the door, then reached out and knocked politely. When no one answered, he opened it and stepped inside.

The first thing he saw was that Caleb *had* broken the stairs. A huge crack ran down the middle of them, so that they tilted crazily in all directions. It was possible to climb them, maybe, if you were very, very careful, but no one would be running down them again.

Grayson stopped in the foyer. The house was dark, with the blinds drawn against the bright, sunny morning.

"Hello?" he called. "Mr. Bowltre? I'd like to talk to you. I'd like to maybe…"

He didn't know what to say. That he wanted to help? How was he supposed to help an adult?

He's here, his wand said suddenly.

And he was. Without warning, Mr. Bowltre appeared from thin air, standing right in front of Grayson. His huge eyes glared and he reached out and grabbed Grayson by one arm, pulling his face close to his own.

"Thief!" he barked.

Chapter 53

Grayson was stiff from fear.

"Let him go!"

He heard Sophia shout from behind him. The others had come through the door.

"Stay back," Grayson said. He tried to keep his voice from trembling.

Out of the corner of his eye, he saw Mr. Bowltre raise his misshapen hand, the Evil Master Wand jutting out from it.

"We can help you," Grayson said to him. "We can make it so that you can think again."

Mr. Bowltre snarled.

"It's not working," Caleb said. "Let me—"

"No! Please, give me a minute." Grayson turned his attention back to the drooling Mr. Bowltre. "We don't want to hurt you. We can—"

Mr. Bowltre made a wet, hacking, coughing laugh. "Hurt me? Boy. Hurt me? No. Hurt you. Hurt and hurt and hurt…" He trailed off, then an even more crazy look came into his eyes. "Give it to me!" he spat.

"Give you what?" Grayson asked.

"Wand. The wand. *My* wand. Give it to me!"

He let go of Grayson but held the Evil Master Wand pointed at Grayson's head. Grayson didn't try to move.

How had Mr. Bowltre appeared from thin air? He had been invisible, like he had used the Invisibility Wand. Only that wand was safe back at the clubhouse. And little sparks were popping at the end of the Evil Master Wand now, like tiny lightning bolts.

I was afraid of this, Grayson's wand said.

"Mr. Bowltre, please—" Grayson tried.

But the hunchbacked man was beyond listening. His strong hands spun Grayson around and grabbed the wand sticking out of his pocket.

There was a tremendous flash, like when he had grabbed Adam's gate, and Mr. Bowltre yelped like a kicked dog. He dropped Grayson's wand and reeled backward but stopped abruptly with a snarl.

"Wicked!" he barked. "Mine!"

Grayson knew he had failed in his attempt to reason with him. Mr. Bowltre was well beyond that point. He bent down and picked up his wand and held it aloft.

Mr. Bowltre snarled, aimed his wand, and unleashed a crack of lightning. It crashed to a halt in front of Grayson with a splatter of brilliant light.

"Wicked!" he howled again.

He pointed at Jonah this time, and Jonah's fingers started to weep water in huge droplets. But after a second, it stopped.

Grayson felt tired.

"Are you helping me?" he asked his wand.

Yes. But it's hard. My counterpart is fighting me. I can't hold on for long. Not against this. You must do something.

Grayson didn't know what to do. He glanced back at Caleb. Caleb returned his look, then nodded and stepped forward.

He drew his wand from his pocket and aimed it at Mr. Bowltre. Sam stepped up beside him and did the same.

Suddenly, Grayson knew what Caleb was going to do.

Don't let him break it! his wand cried. *It's too dangerous!*

"Caleb, don't—" Grayson started, but it was too late.

Caleb's lips moved, but he didn't say anything out loud. Another lightning bolt barely missed him, but he never flinched or took his eyes off of Mr. Bowltre.

Grayson turned back in horror, waiting to see the Evil Master Wand break in two, terrified of what would be unleashed.

Instead, a small, red line appeared in Mr. Bowltre's hand. It was like a paper cut, but it quickly grew larger.

Then, the skin around the Evil Master Wand parted, and Mr. Bowltre howled in pain.

Sam clenched her jaw and pointed her wand. For a moment nothing else happened, but then, with a horrible squelching noise, the Evil Master Wand ripped free of Mr. Bowltre's hand and clattered to the floor.

Instantly Mr. Bowltre went crazy. He howled again and lunged forward, but his bad leg caught behind him and he sprawled to the floor.

Sophia took the opportunity and hid the wand, while Jonah pumped out dark cloud after dark cloud to surround Mr. Bowltre.

He wasn't finished, though. He climbed to his hands and knees and put his face close to the floor, sniffing along it like a dog on the scent of a rabbit.

The Evil Master Wand wanted to be with Mr. Bowltre. It was calling to him and trying to push through Sophia's spell.

But Grayson's wand was fighting back. It was making Sophia's more powerful at the same time as it was trying to counter the Evil Master Wand. And to do all that, it was drawing on Grayson.

He began to sway, feeling more exhausted by the second.

But Mr. Bowltre was slowing down. Whatever rage and madness had propelled him was running out. The Evil Master Wand was using him to pull strength from, as well. He climbed wearily to his feet and glared at them all.

He growled and muttered something they couldn't hear.

Then, he fell over, flat on his face.

Chapter 54

Grayson flopped down to sit on the floor. He was utterly exhausted. But Mr. Bowltre was out cold. *He* lay on the floor without moving; not even snores coming from him.

"Is he dead?" Jonah asked.

"No." Grayson shook his head. "He's just really tired." He yawned. "Like I am."

"Leave him for now," Caleb said. "Let's see if we can help Adam and the others."

Grayson wearily climbed to his feet with Jonah's help, and they followed the others into the dining room. The four adults were still seated around the table, as still as the statues they had been changed into. Bowls of dry cereal were in front of each of them, as well as one that had been half-eaten which was next to June's.

"All right, Sam," Caleb said. "Get the Change Wand?"

"I can't," she said. "It just occurred to me that to do that, I have to use my wand. As soon as I grab the Change Wand, it's going to hurt!"

"Bring it to me," Grayson said quietly.

"I don't know if I can do that," she protested.

"Of course, you can," he replied. "You bring things to you all the time without catching them. Some are just too big, right? So you just put them where you want. Put the Change Wand in my hand."

Sam looked unsure, but finally, she nodded, pointed her wand, and closed her eyes.

Grayson made sure his wand was in his back pocket and held out an open hand. A moment later, another wand was in it, and he closed his fingers around it.

There was no pain, or flash of light, or anything, really. It just felt like a hard piece of wood.

"Can you help me with this?" he asked his wand.

Yes. But you already know what to do, came the answer. *Point it at them. Tell it what you want. The wand will do the rest.*

Grayson pointed the Change Wand at the table. Nothing happened, and he didn't feel anything different.

Because you're not telling it what you want them to be, his wand said.

What I want them to be? Grayson didn't want them to be anything. He just wanted them to be able to be themselves.

A rush of power went through him. He felt it come from his chest and his stomach and his head. His hand trembled but he kept it pointed at the four figures around the table.

It's hard, his wand said. *The Change Wand is used to Nicholas Bowltre now. But I'm trying to get it to…*

Grayson's eyes were fluttering. His hand wavered and he felt like he was going to pass out.

Ah. He thought he heard his wand say something but he really wasn't sure.

"I can't do any…" he muttered.

He sat down heavily, then dropped onto his back, his eyes already closed.

Chapter 55

When Grayson woke up, he heard voices. Not just the voices of his friends, but other ones as well. Deeper voices, like those of adults.

He was still horribly tired and wanted to just keep lying where he was, but Caleb noticed his eyes had opened.

"Hey! You're awake! About time!"

Grayson grinned in response to his friend's teasing. He slowly sat up and looked around.

"How are you feeling, Grayson?" a gentle voice asked him.

Adam was back in his chair. He moved over near Grayson, who saw that his legs had returned to the wooden stumps they had been. But he smiled when he saw Grayson's disappointment.

"Sam was kind enough to get the chair for me," he explained. "My legs are like this from holding onto a wand for too long, not because of anything Nick did. Maybe, someday, I'll find a way to reverse it."

"I'm feeling better," Grayson said. "But I'm sorry. I tried."

"You did more than anyone could have asked of you." Adam raised his voice. "You all did. You should be very proud of yourselves."

Grayson looked beyond Adam to the other adults in the room. Mr. Bowltre was sitting in a chair and June, her spiked hair colored purple and red, was tending to the cut in his hand, but she was talking sharply to him. Mr. Bowltre didn't look at her. He kept his head down and nodded every now and then.

Abigail approached Adam and smiled at Grayson. "Are you sure about this?" she asked Adam.

"I am," he replied, then he turned back to Grayson. "I'm going to take Nick with me. Back to my house. Maybe I can help him." He stopped and regarded Grayson. "That was what you wanted too, wasn't it?"

"He seemed sick," Grayson shrugged. "I don't think he meant to do the things he did."

"Yes, he did," a gruff voice said. Jerry was leaning against a wall, but now he pushed himself forward and shot a glance at Mr. Bowltre. "No one told him to steal wands and shoot me with a lightning bolt. We all knew what we were doing, including him." He looked at around at all the kids.

"And now that I know you're all okay, I'm leaving. Don't call me, Adam. Any of you."

With that, he stalked from the room, and Grayson heard the front door open. There was the crack of a board breaking and a loud curse, and then Jerry was gone.

"Well, I guess we can't all be so forgiving," Adam said quietly. "But what of you? What will you all do now?"

"Go back to the clubhouse," Caleb said instantly. "We still have something to take care of."

"Your parents, of course." Adam smiled. "I wish you luck with that. I would help if I could, but I think my days of holding a wand are over. I'll keep the book, though, for a little while anyway. Long enough to see if I can find an answer for my legs… and for Nick."

"What about his wand?" Sophia asked. "I still have it hidden in the foyer."

"I'll take it," Adam said. "And keep it safe. But I won't be using it."

Grayson wasn't sure if that was smart, but he did know that he didn't want to be responsible for the Evil Master Wand. If Adam said he could keep it safe and away from Mr. Bowltre or anyone else, then he could deal with it.

"Let's go, then," Caleb said. He stopped and looked at Adam for a few seconds, before bending down and hugging him fiercely.

"I'll see you soon," Adam laughed as he patted Caleb's back. "Just because I don't have a wand doesn't mean you're not welcome in my home."

For a short time, at least, Grayson thought. But that was okay.

After they got back to the clubhouse, they'd all have homes again, anyway.

Chapter 56

"Ready?" Caleb asked.

It had taken them awhile to figure out which wand was the Forget Wand, but with the help of Grayson's, they'd managed it.

"How do we do this?" Grayson asked.

"I think we just hold it and tell it what we need," Sam said. "Like you did with the Change Wand."

All the other wands were safely hidden. They'd kept Mr. Bowltre's coat, put the Change Wand back into its loop, and Sophia had hidden the whole thing. They weren't sure what to do with all the wands, but they'd figure that out over the next several days.

For now, they had something more important to do.

"On the count of three," Jonah said.

They stood in a circle and all had a grip on the wand, which was pointing straight up in-between them.

Grayson closed his eyes. He didn't need his wand to help him this time. He had his friends.

It didn't feel like anything, really, but after a few seconds, he opened his eyes and found his friends doing the same.

"Did it work?" he asked.

"I hope so," Caleb said.

"There's only way to find out." Sophia let go of the Forget Wand and pulled her own from her shirt. She pointed it to the side of the clubhouse and suddenly, the wall was gone. In its place was the rest of the basement, with a washer, dryer, furnace, and, most importantly, a set of stairs.

"I hid it all because it was too hard to see it. . ." she said quietly. "The way upstairs where my Mom wouldn't remember me.

She hesitated, took a deep breath, and started toward them.

"Should we wait?" Sam asked.

"I'm not," Grayson decided. "I'm going home. I'll see you all… tomorrow?"

"Why not?" Caleb grinned. "It's still summer."

Grayson smiled back, took one last look at his friends, and ran up the stairs, across the lawn and back to the street. He knew the way now, but even if he hadn't, he still had his wand.

As he neared his house, he slowed. What if they didn't remember him? What if he walked into the house and they didn't even see him?

The idea grew stronger in his mind as he got closer. He still hadn't seen a single other kid in the neighborhood. Not anywhere along the way. So he knew that everything hadn't changed.

When he reached the front door, he stopped. His heart was pounding and his hand was sweaty. The doorknob felt slippery.

Slowly, he turned it and walked in. It occurred to him that he didn't even know what day it was. If it wasn't a weekend, his dad wouldn't be home. But his mom should be.

He could hear her, humming to herself in the kitchen. The aroma of something baking… cookies! … floated out to him.

Grayson walked to the kitchen and stood in the doorway. There she was, just taking a pan out of the oven. His vision blurred and he wiped at his eyes. She didn't notice him after all.

Then…

She glanced over at him and smiled. "Hi honey. Having a good day?"

Grayson almost collapsed with relief. Instead, he blinked hard, cleared his throat, and said, "Yeah. Best I've had in a while."

Epilogue

It had whispered to Adam the whole way back to his house. Abigail had handed him the Evil Master Wand— as Grayson had called it— with a look of disgust and now walked behind him, pushing his chair. It was good to see her again. June, too, of course, but especially Abigail.

You can have it all, the wand whispered. *All the wands. All the magic.*

Adam smiled grimly and ignored the whisperings. They were lies. All he needed to do was look down at his legs to know that.

Once home, June and Nick cleared some things from the stairs and then she led him up to get settled in one of the long-unused bedrooms. Adam went into his library and sighed as he looked at the mess.

"I'll help you," Abigail told him.

"Thank you," he replied. "I hope you'll stay for dinner."

"We'll see," she said, but the small smile gave him hope that she would.

He pushed his chair to a shelf with some books still left on it and moved one of them, uncovering a small, locked safe. He dialed the combination and let the door spring open.

All of it. Anything you want, the wand promised.

"Shut up," Adam muttered.

He put the Evil Master Wand inside, closed the door firmly and locked it. Then, he turned back into the room and set about cleaning up.

The next morning, he was hard at work searching the book, *"The Lost Wands,"* when he came across something that made him gasp.

"No. Oh, no," he breathed.

He hurried over to the shelf and opened the safe.

It was as he'd feared. The Evil Master Wand wasn't there.

It was loose in the world again, and this time, who knew where it was going to end up?

About the Author

James Maxstadt lives in Burlington, NC, where he spends a lot of his time writing books and making wands. He believes magic is real, wand or not, and all you have to do to find it is close your eyes and dream, read a good book, or play a game that you make up the rules for.